RECK

MW01205439

"If you think that being arrested without evidence or probable cause can't happen to you, think again. Julie Bigg Veazey has assembled a cast of opportunists and victims who could hang or redeem themselves. *Reckless Indifference* is a searing indictment of the abusive power of one corrupt individual over another person's life. The story builds to a gripping crescendo as you alternately love and hate the characters."

Robert Henderson, ***Boston Book Club***

"In the capable hands of Julie Bigg Veazey, *Reckless Indifference* becomes a cleverly constructed legal yarn about the unjust targeting of a guiltless man and his battle against the very law that was designed to protect the innocent. It is an engrossing read that winds through the bureaucracy of our legal system as the intertwined actions of the characters irrevocably change the lives of both the innocent and the guilty. The most frightening aspect of the book is: There but for the grace of God go I."

Cheryl Brown, ***Atlantic Book Club***

"Weaving an emotional shuttle through circumstances that evoke a passion for justice, this novel leaves you with a gnawing need for the truth that escapes in the tatters of Eric's unraveling life. *Reckless Indifference* explores an intricate net of lies and how they eventually ensnare the spinner. Once again, Julie Bigg Veazey's characters, through vivid dialog and action, envelop the reader with a scary look at reality."

Robert Leigh Meek, ***Chemistry of Power***

"Inconceivably, the destiny of a flawed but hard-working husband and father becomes determined by an ambitious beat cop who fabricates one reckless untruth which leads to another and another until three states are involved in an entaglement of deceit. With fascinating perception into each character, the author leads the story into legal recourse, tragedy, and redemption."

Barbara DeWall, ***Arizona Review***

Reckless Indifference

for Donna & Alan
Enjoy!

Julie Bigg Veazey

a novel by **Julie Bigg Veazey**

author of *Silent Cry*

Booksurge Publishing
North Charleston, South Carolina

Reckless Indifference is a work of fiction based loosely on actual events. Names, characters, places, and incidents have been changed through the author's imagination or are used fictitiously. Any resemblance to actual events, locales, or persons, living or dead, is entirely coincidental and not intended by the author.

ISBN: 1-4392-0325-3
ISBN-13: 9781439203255
Library of Congress Control Number: 2008907307

Cover Design: Elan Alexenberg
Author Photograph: Elan Alexenberg

To contact the author, e-mail: juliebvz@yahoo.com

Booksurge Publishing
North Charleston, South Carolina

Printed in the United States of America

Acknowledgments:

My unceasing thanks to my husband Bill for his honesty and integrity in reviewing *Reckless Indifference,* and enormous appreciation goes to my loyal and discerning readers: Shary, Stevie, Bobby, Lynn, Dan, Cheryl, Mickey, Sharon, Medi, Steve, and Mary.

To my brother, I give my love and special recognition for the inspiration and the encouragement to write this book.

Praise and gratitude go to my editors, Mary Linn Roby, Pagan Kennedy, and Merle Drown, who empowered and inspired me to greater heights than I thought possible, and to Lynn Rockwell who, with incredible attention to detail, put the final touches on *Reckless Indifference.*

To Bill,

You encouraged me with unswerving support,

and look what happened—

another novel!

I thank you with all my heart.

Reckless Indifference:

"The conscious disregard of the consequences of one's acts or omissions against the protected legal rights of an aggrieved individual."

Wikipedia / New Jersey Law

PROLOGUE

It was time to begin. They couldn't be more ready. Six months working in that boring, claustrophobic print shop had been training enough for her.

She had chosen her materials carefully, taking time to find out-of-the-way stationery stores around the city where she could get the perfect paper for price tags. As for the ink, she had bought one cartridge at a time along Varick Street in Tribeca. The printer had been another problem entirely. She had actually driven all the way down to Maryland before finding just the right price-tag printer sitting idle and dusty in the back of a used-equipment store.

J.P. had worked with a gemologist for three years before they met, and together they had come up with the idea. Well, in truth, it had been her idea, but she gave him the credit. It wasn't a crazy, get-rich-fast scheme, but one she knew would succeed because of their discipline and anonymity. She had drilled into him that they could not be greedy, that it was the one thing that would cause their downfall. Having grown up in Briar Cliff Manor, she had seen what greed could do to people.

They had done their homework well, casing security set-ups in various chain stores before choosing one that would work for them, a store where they had actually made purchases. Always be careful to shop alone, she had cautioned J.P., and pay cash, of course. Too bad that he was annoyed with her repeated instructions; they couldn't be too careful.

Anticipation jumped in the pit of her stomach. Granddad could go to hell with all his money. She wouldn't need it after this.

Initially, she and J.P. had agreed to work solo. However, at the last minute, they had realized that there was one more link needed to make their plan work—a trusted fence who could move the product—and there he sat now across the room slumped down in an easy chair just waiting for them to begin. Where J.P. had ever found him was beyond her imagining. But he'd have to do because they had already set a date. And this was only the beginning.

* * *

CHAPTER ONE

Even though Saturdays at the Gordon's in Parkdale, New Jersey brought in many "lookers," Mary felt excited when a man approached her fine jewelry counter just before lunchtime that memorable day. She just knew she was going to make a sizable sale, particularly when he stopped in front of the diamond rings. In his late thirties, dark-haired and sharply dressed in slate gray pants and a navy sport jacket, this guy obviously had good taste. She'd put a jacket like his on layaway for her Jimmy.

"I'd like to see some engagement rings, miss," he said. There was something so gracious about him that Mary was immediately impressed.

After placing a tray of engagement rings on the counter, Mary watched him carefully, as she had been instructed during her training sessions in New York. She could smell his aftershave which was nothing like Jimmy's Old Spice. His smelled strong and expensive. And she noticed the French cuffs of his shirt held large gold cuff links that were studded with diamonds.

There was one ring that he seemed particularly interested in. Glancing down at the chart under the counter, Mary noted that the ring he held had a center oval-cut 1.73 carat diamond set in a yellow-gold Tiffany mounting. It had fine color and clarity. He kept studying the price tag. It was amusing that he was probably trying to figure out the wholesale code, but she knew he never could. Even her boss didn't know how to do that. Just when she thought he was on the verge of buying, he replaced the ring on the tray, pulled down on each cuff and straightened his tie. "Thank you, miss," he said to Mary. "I'm pretty sure my fiancée will like it, but she has to be the one to give the thumbs-up." She knew what that meant. He wouldn't be back.

At about quarter of five that afternoon, much to Mary's surprise, in came the same man, this time accompanied by a young, spiffy-looking, well-dressed blonde, and an older man who seemed to be with them but stood back passively. Maybe his father. Or hers? He was far from attractive and when he grinned at her, she noticed that most of his teeth were missing. Or that's what she thought she saw.

"I'd like to look at that ring again, miss, if you don't mind," the young man said, smiling broadly at Mary.

Pulling the tray from the case, Mary nearly told him that she had had a feeling that he'd come back but instead she placed the ring he had looked at before in the middle of the black velvet pad on the counter.

"It's so beautiful, isn't it," she said, "and the stone is of the highest quality."

The young woman beamed at her fiancé as she slid it on her finger. You could tell they were in love.

"May I take a look at it in the natural light over there by the window?" she asked Mary.

"Certainly," Mary responded, maybe too quickly. She glanced over at her boss to be sure it was okay and was relieved when he gave a reassuring nod.

The couple headed for the large plate-glass window at the front of the store about twenty feet away, followed by the older man who took the ring from her and, holding it up to the light, stared at it through a jeweler's loupe. After what seemed like a long time, he frowned and muttered something that Mary could not possibly hear although she tried, and then the two customers returned to the counter, while the older man started toward the exit.

"It certainly is a beauty," the young man commented, as he placed the ring back on the velvet pad. "I was sure she'd like it," he said sheepishly.

"I'm truly sorry," the woman told Mary, "but it just doesn't seem right for me."

Mary could tell that they were feeling badly about the situation—uncomfortable, too. She sensed the shift in their enthusiasm and felt disappointed for them, a bit more than for herself. She knew, however, that it wasn't her place to say anything. That's another thing they taught you in New York; never try to push a customer into a sale. Although, personally, she couldn't imagine any woman turning down a diamond of such quality and brilliance. And almost two carats.

"Sorry," the young woman repeated over her shoulder as she headed for the door, followed by her fiancé. Mary loved the sound of her spike heels clicking across the tiled floor. She could never wear shoes like that, being on her feet all day.

When Mary glanced at her boss, he shrugged and nodded as though to tell her that these things happen. Someday, she thought, she would be choosing an engagement ring too, although, of course, not in that price range. Actually, Jimmy had suggested that they put matching sterling wedding bands on layaway and then, maybe at some anniversary in the future, he could replace hers with a real diamond set in gold.

It was difficult for her to understand why the woman hadn't loved such a gorgeous ring, and, just for fun, Mary tried it on and held it to the light. She hadn't expected it to feel that natural on her finger, or to sparkle so. Suddenly she saw her boss frowning at her from his counter across the aisle. Remembering the clear no-no from her training session when it came to trying on the merchandise, she quickly placed the ring back on the tray. Gordon's had taken a chance on her, being so young, and she wasn't about to disappoint them.

* * *

CHAPTER TWO

Eric knew Shelly couldn't stand to hear him beg so he kept his mouth shut. Staring out the window through the darkness, he could just make out the silhouette of their old gray Pontiac next to the new BMW which Shelly had pushed so hard for. They were the last family on the street to buy a new car.

"Too bad if this isn't what you want," she told him.

"You knew we hadn't been happy for a while," he said plaintively, reaching to touch her shoulder. "She never meant anything to me."

"She!" Shelly spit out, slapping his hand away. "As if you had just one affair."

"It was only once, I swear," he protested as she stalked across the living room, her footsteps silent on the oriental carpet.

She turned her back to him. "It doesn't matter how many times or with whom. I don't want to know. I just want you gone. We both need time."

A sharp silence cut between them. The walls of the house seemed to be closing in, squeezing him out of where he belonged. He heard Jason and Arthur roughhousing upstairs. Normally he would be calling up to them to settle down and do their homework. This life, this family was something he and Shelly had created and built together and now she was putting an end to it.

Blinking away tears that were blurring his vision behind his wire-rimmed glasses, Eric strode across the room to stand directly in front of her. Usually when he looked down at her, she would reach up and coax his straight dark bangs back and to the side—a tender touch that was definitely not about to happen now. He hated the way she looked just past him when they argued, as though he were in another room.

"Shelly, look at me," he said. "I know there's no excuse for what I did but I swear it'll never happen again."

"No, Eric."

"Please, for God's sake Shel, if nothing else, think of the boys. This is going to kill them."

"You think it isn't killing me?" She stared at the floor, her face set in the hard lines that he had put there, and heaved a long drawn-out sigh. "If you want to, we can just consider it a trial separation."

"I suppose you're picturing me in a cozy little apartment around the corner," Eric said.

"It does make sense that *you* move out, Eric. Because of the boys. I mean—so their lives will remain constant."

"Yes, but what about *my* life? I work an hour and a half away." Eric's heart was beginning to race. Not to be able *or allowed* to go home after a sales trip or a long day in the office was unimaginable.

"You should've thought about that before," she hissed. "And keep your voice down, will you? I don't want the boys to hear us."

"Oh yeah, what do you propose to tell them?" He hated confrontation.

"We can arrange all of that, Eric. Calm down. I just need time alone."

"Alone? You mean so you can look for someone to replace me? How the hell can I be calm when you are pulling the rug out from under me—taking away all the things I really care about, consigning me to some hole-in-the-wall room while you carry on, life as usual?"

Sniffing loudly, Shelly reached for a tissue, balled it in her fist, and folded her arms across her chest. Her lower lip was drawn in, a habit Eric recognized as meaning that the last word had been said on the subject.

Suddenly, he needed to get out of there. He couldn't take another minute of her pouring on the guilt. He'd said he was sorry, and he really was, but no one's perfect. Without waiting any longer for a response, Eric began rushing around the living room, randomly collecting family photos. He knew he was acting irrationally; so differently than his usual methodical engineer's demeanor, but he didn't give a damn at this point. She just stood there watching. God only knows what she was thinking, as he lifted his clarinet case off one of the shelves of the large cherry entertainment center that they had bought in an antique shop, that he had spent months refinishing in the garage. When he got to the hallway, Eric pulled the front door open with such force that it banged against the wall, something he had told the boys over and over not to do.

Pausing in the yard, Eric looked back at Shelly who was standing in the doorway, the chill wind lifting her hair. Leaves, already dropping from the maples that lined the street, scuttled along the sidewalk. The scent of ochre mums Eric had planted last year rose to mingle with his sadness.

"Please take the Pontiac, Eric," Shelly called. "I'd like the BMW. For the kids' sake," she added. Her tone told him that she felt a little ashamed for asking. *But not enough to stop her.*

Eric sprinted across the yard, brittle with early frost, threw his things in the back seat of the Pontiac, and slammed the door.

"What about your clothes?" he heard Shelly call after him.

"I'll get them later," he shouted back at her, as he revved the engine and roared out of the driveway, away from Tolleson, New Jersey, only twenty miles northwest of New York City, the upper middle-class neighborhood Shelly had wanted so badly. When he took a sharp corner, a baseball that one of the boys had left in the car thumped across the back floor.

As he drove on watching for a motel, Eric tried to change radio stations, forgetting that he hadn't had the antenna fixed yet because he wanted the goddamn car-wash people to pay for it. Hours later, he was still driving around aimlessly, unable to really think of anything except the way Shelly had looked, framed in the open doorway.

He knew that the personal events that alter one's life could usually be dated to a specific point in time. Until this night, the Nordblums had lived their lives in a single shade of color, a mild tone of light blue, like a blank computer screen. Now he had come to a turning point and everything ahead looked black.

* * *

CHAPTER THREE

Oh God, Mary thought, how she hated taking inventory every ninety days, as if things were going to change in-between time. She kept a running inventory as items were sold and new stock came in, so these physical inventories seemed a waste of time to her.

When she spotted a well-dressed man weaving purposefully through the store right toward her counter, she assumed correctly that it was the new specialist from New York.

"Jason Goldberg," he said, raising his hand in a salute. He was a small man, standing stiffly erect as though trying to appear taller. And important. It was obvious that he was not offering to shake hands with her.

"Pleased to meet you. I'm Mary Fletcher."

As they began the process, Mary actually felt a little afraid of him, as though at any minute he might jump down her throat about something she had done wrong. After she made a tray count, he wanted the same tray to be brought to him so that he might check it personally. She had heard in the lunchroom that this was his first inspection, so obviously he was anxious to do a flawless job. She could certainly sympathize with that, but he didn't need to act quite so cocky.

Using a jeweler's loupe, he chose at random one piece of jewelry after another and examined them closely. He was really dragging out the process, probably showing off, and Mary had already been on her feet for hours. As long as he was there, no sale would be made. She couldn't imagine what he was looking for since she knew her stock, and was positive everything was in order. Sneaking a look at her watch, she saw that it was past time for her to go home.

He brought one diamond ring up close to his eye. "What's this?" he demanded suddenly, frowning at Mary. "This must be from the costume counter."

"No, sir, it's from *this* counter."

"Well, obviously there's some mistake," he responded, as he slipped his loupe into his breast pocket. "Take a look for yourself," he said, extending the diamond toward her as though it was poisonous. Her hand trembled ever so slightly when she reached under the counter for her loupe. Initially, the stone looked fine to her, so she looked closer, examined each facet, and how the stone was set. Flaws began to appear and slowly the realization of what she was looking at sunk in. Mary felt herself going numb. Something terrible was happening—she could feel danger running along her spine.

"You're right, it doesn't belong here." Her voice was barely audible.

Jesus, Mary, and Joseph, that's the ring I tried on . . .

"Take it over to costume. Let's do an immediate recount."

Mary knew it wasn't her who'd screwed things up. Maybe the part-time woman—she didn't have as much at stake in this job. She was suddenly overcome by the feeling of her weight settling and everything around her dropping into slow motion. The usual stream of customers and their chatter that normally excited her, made her hopeful, receded into a steady hum that buzzed in the back of her head.

It didn't take long to determine that nothing was missing from the costume counter.

"I just spoke to your boss," Jason said. "He told me to send you home now. He wants to check every single fine piece himself. I've got to notify New York." His eyes looked suddenly weary.

Mary had a feeling that this was going to turn out to be something awful. In a way, she kind of pitied Jason being on his first inspection. It wasn't his fault, but at the same time, it was nothing that she did; of that she was sure. Still, she prayed it wouldn't be hung on her.

Grateful to be leaving, she unlocked her car and slid onto the cold seat and watched the darkness grow beyond the frost-crazed window; how it hid the field beyond and swallowed the nearly barren trees of mid-November that edged the empty parking lot.

She started the car. Cold seeped into her bones while she waited for it to warm up. If she lost her job, she'd lose the wedding rings they had on layaway, and how would she handle the loan of five thousand yet to be paid on this Nissan which she loved even though it had 60,000 miles? Maybe she'd even lose Jimmy. And there would be no recommendation for another jewelry store job, which was the only thing she was trained to do. She forced herself to leave the lot and head home.

The city lights showed weakly; pale heartless flickers at the fringe of the hard silence within the car. Mary slowed when she passed Jimmy's house, craning to see if his bedroom light was on. They both still lived at home in order to save money for their wedding. That had been her idea and even though Jimmy was reluctant, he'd agreed.

She dreaded going home. She was never able to hide anything from her mother. And if she lost her job over this, *something she didn't do*, there'd be no more special little surprises for her parents. Not that they expected anything in the way of rent, but she found the prospect of her not being able to give them gifts enormously depressing.

Water dripped off the roof and landed inside the collar of her coat, running down her back when she bent to unlock the door. She heard her mother in the kitchen, singing cheerfully, and there was nothing Mary wanted more than to get back into her car and keep driving.

※ ※ ※

The waiting area in the Parkdale police station was buzzing with people, all of whom ignored Mary. She sat on a wooden bench clasping her hands tightly on her lap. Along the opposite wall was a gallery of ominous photographs of most-wanted people, only one of whom was a woman. She felt tears well in the corners of her eyes. The self-assured looking men in suits had to be lawyers. *Do I need a lawyer?* She watched as an older man, handcuffed and stinking of booze, was being led down a scary-looking corridor by a uniformed cop. Probably to a jail cell. And speaking of smells, a girl no older than Mary sat farther down the bench in sleazy-looking clothes drenched in such cheap perfume that it was making her nauseous.

She was working herself up to near panic. What if they checked her background and somehow found out that Jimmy was driving without a license. Worse than that, were they planning to frame her for this robbery? She pressed on her knee to stop her foot from jiggling like an old-fashioned sewing machine.

When someone asked if she was Miss Fletcher, Mary jumped to her feet, clutching her purse to her chest.

"Follow me," a man said. "I'm Detective Cushman and this is Mickey, our sketch artist," he added, as they entered a small room where a young man rose from the table behind which he had been seated and smiled at her reassuringly.

"So, we understand from your boss that you were working the jewelry counter when the thieves switched the ring," the detective said, offering her a seat. "Right?"

"Well, at least I *think* it was them. It had to be them because it certainly wasn't me." Mary hardly recognized her own voice. There were no windows in this room. How could they stand it? She remembered when she broke her wrist in gym class and was so scared at the hospital that they gave her a brown paper bag to breathe into. She might need one now.

"No one's accusing you of anything," the detective told her. "We just want a description so that Mick here can draw up a picture for circulation. You do want us to catch the bad guys. Right, Miss Fletcher?"

"Of course," she said. "Why wouldn't I?" She had to stop herself from thinking about Jimmy or she would burst into sobs. And if she did, they'd probably think she was guilty. An intercom suddenly blared in the hallway paging an Officer Nathan so loudly that she could hear it through the closed door. The room was getting horribly stuffy.

"Okay. When word went out to all the Gordon's stores that several locations were also missing engagement rings, that rang a bell for you. Right?"

"Yes." Oh, how she had hated drawing attention to herself, but she had felt an obligation to Gordon's to mention the episode that had occurred at her counter several weeks ago. And now, because of her loyalty, she was here being interrogated. Maybe even arrested.

"What was the value of the ring that's missing?"

"Eight thousand," Mary responded so softly that the detective had to lean closer in order to hear. She cringed at the thought that even though she had gone through the New York training, she hadn't had a clue that the diamond was a fake. And to think that she had actually tried it on and watched it sparkle—thought it was gorgeous.

She told the police exactly what had happened, as she remembered it. The artist hesitated after each of her descriptions and then sketched furiously with his No. 2 pencil. The heat from the gooseneck light curved over the paper he was drawing on was making him sweat. She was too.

The detective seemed pleased after she added details such as the fact that the younger man wore diamond-studded cuff links and the possibility that the woman's hair looked so perfect that it could even have been a wig. She also mentioned that she thought the older man was missing some teeth. But the detective's relaxed friendliness did not dispel her fear.

Should she tell that she tried on the ring? Would her boss tell the police anyway? And would it implicate her?

✳ ✳ ✳

CHAPTER FOUR

At the end of the work day, exhausted, Eric had been on his way to his car when he saw a sign advertising an apartment for rent nailed to a telephone pole. What the hell, he thought. He might as well check it out, particularly since the address turned out to be right in Dalton, only three blocks from his office, and now, dressed in a rumpled suit and tie, his winter coat still in the car, he stood on the top step of the wraparound porch and let the landlady scrutinize him. He felt a biting wind whip up and snap his pants back and forth against his legs.

After a moment she stuck out her hand, palm up. "I'd like to see your driver's license first, please," she said. Shading his eyes, he glanced past her into the large entrance hall and up the steep stairwell. The place reminded him of Grammie Nordblum's house where he had gone to live when he was fourteen.

"Thanks," the woman announced, handing Eric back his license. She was smiling now as she invited him inside and up the creaky stairs. "I rent three small apartments here and my daughter and I live on the other side of the house. The second floor is the one that's available," she explained.

Eric followed, hating that Shelly had banished him from their house. The house he was paying for, and would be for years to come, was miles away in New Jersey—with his boys in it, doubtless wondering what had happened to their father. He hadn't had the opportunity yet to explain anything to them or what they could expect, but he was sure that Shelly had already fed them her side of the story.

The apartment consisted of a small living room with an alcove that was set up as an office, complete with a wooden desk and a rickety metal bookshelf. The bedroom was even smaller, with a single mattress that resembled a canoe. The entire apartment was painted a dingy beige. A clean-looking bathroom was around the corner with only a shower and a pink toilet and sink dating from the '50s. There was a separate kitchenette with a table for two. He didn't like eating alone, even when he was traveling. The musty smell was just like the basement apartment he lived in while working for his master's degree in Electrical Engineering. Back in the living room, Eric opened the shade, brittle with age, covering the only window, and looked out at the driveway where a basketball net lay in the grass. It made him heartsick to think that this would be his view for who knew how long. At least it was close to his office. He could even walk it. *How pathetic is that, looking for something positive in all of this?*

"I'd need telephone and internet hookups," Eric told her, listening to the old refrigerator. There was a big round motor on the top, humming away.

I'm not here, he thought. I'm not doing this.

"That stuff is already installed. You'd just have to get your name on it."

When he hesitated to make a comment, she started chattering about the town and how friendly it was.

Jesus, she's telling me about a singles group that meets every other Sunday at the Unitarian church that's within walking distance. What was she, a psychic? And she even has the balls to say that they offered free counseling there. Was he that obvious?

"Okay, I'll take it," Eric interrupted her.

The minute he said the words, there was a sharp pain in his chest, as though he, himself, had plunged a knife there.

* * *

CHAPTER FIVE

Angelo Deluca leaned back in his oversized leather desk chair and propped his feet on the bottom drawer of his file cabinet. He stared at the speakerphone from which his old friend Dan Fortini's voice was booming.

"Morning, how's His Honor doing?" As always when on the phone, Dan tended to sound like a drill sergeant.

"About what you'd expect," Angelo replied, welcoming the break from reading the report about last night's Land Use meeting. "What's up with Radcliff's greatest wop-cop?"

Angelo enjoyed the easiness of the banter with Dan, who had been his chief for seventeen years. There wasn't anything that happened that Dan didn't know about, and Angelo made sure nothing *important* happened without his own approval. That control was essential.

"You're not looking for another raise, are you, *Pizonne?*"

"Cut the shit, Angelo," Dan said, "we're not back at Rutgers on the football field. This is business."

Angelo reached across his desk to straighten the football that sat on the corner in a Lucite holder. Those had been their glory days.

"I just got a call from the manager of that new store over in the mall," Dan was saying, in a voice that the speaker twisted into a squawk.

"Yeah, I met him," Angelo said. "I was at the grand opening ceremony."

He looked at the lineup of photographs on the west wall of his office of him shaking hands with VIPs, his attention focusing on his absolute favorite; Ronald Reagan, wearing that genuine smile that grabbed him every time, the smile that you knew was meant for only you. Dan had missed out being in the photo. He still doesn't get it, that you have to push to get into the spotlight.

"The manager's name is Chad something," Angelo said, turning his attention to the photo taken that opening day. Not a bad shot, he thought, noting how he had successfully managed to maneuver partially behind the manager in order to camouflage his girth.

Angelo regretted having gotten so damned fat. Not long after college, he had become an alderman. Then, after three years on the school board, he had entered local politics with a vengeance. The road to becoming mayor was filled with fund-raising dinners, lots of political bullshit, and—no exercise. It just crept up on him, especially after Agnes died; he mostly ate out. He could, and probably should, go on a diet, but now he had no one to please except Shirley who didn't seem to mind.

"Right. Chad Richardson," Dan replied. "He says that some other Gordon's stores have been robbed and he wants us to stake a cop out at his store. Round-the-clock. He's really steaming."

From his window, Angelo looked down at Radcliff's central green dominated by a Revolutionary War memorial, which he had fought for like a tiger. Dan had backed him on it as well as other grateful citizens. And there still were no parking meters on the main streets, also thanks to him.

"That's pretty goddamned presumptuous," Angelo said tentatively, twisting his chair back to look at the wall behind him where his personal history was displayed: college degree, commendations from one of the Radcliff Boy Scout troops, the governor's council on aging, the Red Cross, and a photo of him and Agnes on their wedding day. The framed snapshot of his son Tony, taken at his high school graduation, sat as though in disgrace on the floor in the corner of his office. The string Agnes had hung it with had broken years ago. Once again, Angelo made a mental note to fix it.

"Are you listening, for Crissake?" Dan sounded more irritated than usual. "This guy is the temporary manager and says he can't move on to the next Gordon's opening with the possibility of a robbery hanging over his head at this one."

Angelo knew Dan would be pacing around his office in the police station. He could almost imagine his face glaring at him from across the green.

"I don't need some store manager telling me what to do," Angelo said, uncovering the carton of his leftover sweet-and-sour chicken and reaching in for one last bite.

"Here's what I'm thinking," Dan said, talking fast. "They won't be dumb enough to pull a heist at yet another Gordon's, so my idea is to plant one of our *best* detectives over at Steacie's Jewelry store; maybe Rick Robbins. I figure if the bastards hit here in Radcliff, it'll be a high-end store, not Gordon's. I'll set up the sting and we'll catch them red-handed at Steacie's."

"Then what will you tell the guy at Gordon's?" Angelo asked him, picturing Dan running his fingers through his overgrown crew cut while he considered his answer.

"Maybe send someone over there just to satisfy his request. What do you think?"

"That's excellent reasoning for a hometown police chief. Why not put Tony on it?"

"Jesus, Angelo, don't you give a shit about this?"

"Of course, everything that happens in Radcliff concerns me. But Dan, I imagine Tony'd love to play detective and get a break from the beat for a while." Angelo remembered how annoying it had been, years ago, when Agnes had placed Tony's silver baby cup on his desk. As a reminder, she had said. Now it was tarnished and filled with paperclips. But it was, nonetheless, still there.

Angelo looked up just as Shirley walked into his office and waved a paper under his nose. *Don't forget you're having dinner with me tonight . . .* There was a little happy face at the end of the note. She picked up the carton of Chinese and left after he winked at her. *Nothing like Agnes, but not bad.*

Thumbing through the notes he had taken at the meeting, it occurred to Angelo that there were certain advantages to confining Dan to a speakerphone, within his control. "Sounds like a plan, buddy," he told Dan. "Keep me informed. Be sure to use Tony. You've been sitting on him long enough."

"If you say so, His Honor," Dan said, not attempting to hide his disapproval.

Angelo knew how to interpret that tone, particularly since Dan was the only living person who knew all of his demons.

Getting to the top hadn't been easy, but staying there—that was the challenge that faced Angelo every day.

* * *

CHAPTER SIX

"Yeah, chief, what's up?" Tony Deluca said when he heard Dan's voice. "I was just heading out. Can we do this later?" Pulling his police cap on over his unruly blond hair, he jiggled the keys in his hand impatiently because he and Bernie were going to Sherman's for lunch.

"No, Tony, we can't do this later," Dan growled over the receiver. "This is important. We've got a situation that's potentially hot."

"What's going on, Chief?" Tony flexed his abs as he often did when no one was watching. Exercise was important, particularly when there was obesity in the family. No one was more conscious of maintaining his weight than Tony. He ignored the fact that Bernie was paging him over the intercom.

"The manager over at Gordon's thinks a jewelry rip-off might be heading their way," Dan told him. "I want you to get your ass over to Bridge Street and keep an eye open. This is the chance you've been waiting for so don't flub it," Dan continued. "Go see Chad Richardson; he's the big cheese there from New York. Tell him we've decided he should allow them to steal whatever and start out the door with it. That's when you play hero."

Tony snapped to attention. Why was the chief telling him this over the phone? After all, his office was just around the corner. "But I heard you were sending Rick Robbins over to Steacie's," he said. There was nothing Tony would like better than to one-up on Rick who had been in his graduating class at the academy.

"Yeah, but I'm sending *you* to Gordon's, where the heist is *really expected.* You'll be pulling off a sting. Have your cell phone ready and tell Richardson to call you as soon as he thinks the sonsabitches have the jewelry. Then you move in and grab 'em right as they exit."

Tony could hardly believe the chief was using him. Maybe "using" was the operative word—maybe he was sending him on a wild-goose chase. Nonetheless, he looked over the five-foot partition that separated his desk from the others to see if anyone was listening. Even though the place was fairly deserted, he sat down and lowered his voice. "Should I take Bernie with me, Chief?"

"No, that's not necessary. You can handle it."

"Okay. When is this coming down?"

"How the hell should I know? Jesus, Tony, just get over there, set up the sting and stay put."

"Got it, boss. I'm on my way. Hey, did His Honor recommend me for this job? Because if he did, tell Pop I've got it covered."

Before leaving, Tony put on his vest and checked his belt, from strong to weak side: speed loaders, sidearm, leatherman, handcuffs over right back pocket, flashlight ring, key ring, Taser, maglight ring, and cell phone in his breast pocket. Clamping down on his holster with his elbow, he told himself he was ready for anything. He could already picture himself in an office of his own with Detective Deluca on the door.

* * *

Actually, Tony had heard something about these robberies, but he hadn't paid much attention since Radcliff hadn't been involved. Now he stopped to scrutinize a composite sent down from the Parkdale police department that had been on the bulletin board for a while. A good-looking guy with dark hair, a blonde who looked like a model, and an ugly sonofabitch. They shouldn't be too hard to pick out.

No doubt about it, he was excited about this assignment, particularly since he figured it might have been his father's idea. Finally he was getting something to sink his teeth into instead of checking two-hour parking violations and hustling drunks off the street.

Tony knew he had disappointed his father in every way imaginable ever since early childhood, especially in anything to do with sports. Thanks to Pop's short temper and heavy hand, Tony had grown up hating to be touched. So there went football. And to this day, he'd always been just a little overweight; not fat, fat, like Pop had become—which didn't matter to him—he'd love His Honor fat or thin, if he'd let him. As long as he could remember, his father, *His-Honor-the-Mayor*, had been the only hero in their house. But now, Tony was goddamn well going to make that change.

* * *

On his way out to Gordon's, Tony turned the flashers on and skidded through slush left from the first snow since Thanksgiving. His stomach grumbled when he spotted

Bernie heading into Sherman's Diner without him. He strained to see what the specials were listed on the billboard out front and then told himself that there was no time for that.

It was about time Pop had gotten around to telling Dan to give him something important to do. Maybe they would finally consider him for full-time detective.

Impatiently, he stopped at a crosswalk in front of Lawrence's store, which used to house the post office, as well as carry anything you might want from hunting gear to Campbell's soup. It reminded him of when he and Bernie spent their allowances on the penny candy. Bernie, who was still his best friend.

Wait'll he hears about this assignment. He knows how I've been busting my chops for something like this.

The bell in Saint Elizabeth's tower tolled noon, a sad reminder that he hadn't been to church since his mother's funeral. She'd be proud when he became a detective, he told himself, as he pulled away from the crosswalk like a greyhound tearing out of the starting gate, speeding past his apartment on Chester Street and spinning out around the circle, heading for the new mall out on Route 4. He enjoyed the way people stopped and stared, obviously wondering where the emergency was as he flew past.

Less than five minutes later, Tony pulled up to the front entrance of Gordon's and got out of the cruiser, leaving the lights flashing.

"Where's the manager," he asked the salesgirl behind the first counter he came to. She pointed.

Following her directions, Tony strode down the cosmetics aisle, making his way past jewelry and on through the lingerie department. He opened the office door without knocking.

"I'm officer, uh . . . Detective Deluca with the Radcliff police," he announced. "I hear that you think you're going to get robbed sometime soon."

For a moment, the tall, intense-looking man at the desk simply blinked at him from behind his horn-rimmed glasses. "Glad you're here," he said finally, spitting the words out like a machine gun. "Thanks for coming so quickly. I'm Chad Richardson. I've launched each new Gordon's location for six years now and I've never had a robbery while I was in charge. And I damn well don't want one now, especially with the Christmas season just starting."

Tony knew his type; buddy-buddy when he wants a favor, then screw-you if he gets caught doing something illegal.

"Your chief said you'd stay with us until something happens, no matter how long it takes." His office had boxes stacked in one corner and piles of clothes, with big tags attached, heaped on a couch, maybe being marked down for sale. But the desk, Tony noticed, was neat as a pin, one pile of folders and a pen lying beside a blank yellow legal pad. Along with a delicious-looking Reuben on the pullout shelf with one bite missing.

"Yes sir, here's the idea." Assuming his most businesslike manner, Tony laid out the plan and gave Chad his cell phone number. "So, as soon as they head for the exit," he summarized briskly, "call me and I'll nab them on the sidewalk. Okay?"

It was clear from Richardson's expression that the idea had impressed him. He read Tony's cell number out loud for confirmation.

"Sounds like a good plan," Chad told him as he walked Tony to the office door. "And I suspect we won't have long to wait, since there was a suspicious-acting guy here a short time ago, asking about engagement rings. So, we want to be ready. Right?"

"Right," Tony answered. *Ugh, bad breath. Maybe he's got a nervous stomach like the chief or it could be the sandwich, which looks extremely tempting.*

Feeling confident, Tony passed back through the store making a vow to himself.

He was going to do his father proud, as well as get in good with the chief.

* * *

CHAPTER SEVEN

An hour and forty minutes later, Tony's phone rang once and Chad's voice pierced the quiet of the squad car: "They're here! They've got a ring and they're heading out the door."

Tony dropped the phone and paused for a split second as twin threads of fear and excitement ran through him. He went still, a quietness on the far side of thinking, as he dropped his hand to his holster. Keeping his eyes riveted on the entrance to Gordon's, he tried to clear his thoughts.

Holy shit. There they were, casually exiting the store. An older guy followed by a normal-looking couple. Normal, but clipping along fast. And there was the manager rushing out behind them.

Jumping out of the car, Tony ran toward Gordon's, at the same time waving at Chad to get back into the store. His legs felt rubbery. The weight of his equipment seemed to multiply, getting heavier with each step during his thirty-foot sprint across the street.

"Stop right there," Tony shouted, already out of breath, his voice several octaves higher than usual. As all three suspects started walking faster, the taller man threw Tony a look over his shoulder that made his heart skip a beat.

"Stop!" Tony yelled, unsnapping his holster as he ran, and drawing his gun. He was afraid they were about to bolt.

"Hands up where I can see them. All of you," he yelled. "I said, *now*."

Freezing indecisively in the middle of the sidewalk, the trio turned around. The woman, looking stunned, started to raise her hands.

Fixating on their movements, Tony reached with his left hand for his cuffs, wishing to hell that he had brought three with him. Now his legs were shaking.

The bullet, sounding like a cannon blast, whistled past Tony. He saw Chad, who had fallen to the sidewalk, reach for his left thigh.

Tony stopped in his tracks and radioed for backup. "Man down at Gordon's," he yelled into his shoulder mic. What should he do next—attend to Chad who was lying on his back, writhing with pain, or pursue the three robbers who were sprinting for their car? Not bothering to respond to questions from dispatch, he shouted: "Pursuing shooter," and took off.

Now in a state of panic, Tony thought about firing off a round as he ran toward their gray Pontiac just after they had piled into the car and started the ignition. The exhaust fumes made his eyes water.

"Stop!" Tony shouted again. Grabbing the antenna, he bent it at a right angle as the car pulled away from the curb. When it picked up speed, he took hold of the door handle, screaming: "Stop, you fuckers!" at the top of his lungs.

Racing alongside the car, he pressed his face against the window as it shot forward. He grabbed the door handle, trying to keep pace with the car, but it was ripped from his grip and he landed just beyond where his gun had fallen in the gutter. Before the car disappeared around the corner,

he got the New York license number. At least he thought
he did.

* * *

Tony saw Chad wince as an EMT stuck a shot into his
arm. Relieved that help had come, he stepped back and
crouched against the building, frantically feeling in his
pockets for a pen. The only piece of paper he could put
his hand on was the Miranda warning card. Desperately
blanking out the hubbub around him, Tony concentrated
on recalling the license number he had been repeating over
and over to himself.

"I demand to see the cop," he heard Chad bark in an
almost demented voice as the stretcher was being lifted
into an ambulance.

"I'm here. I'm right here," Tony answered, making his
way through the crowd of onlookers. *Where had they all come
from?*

"You imbecile, what the hell happened?" Chad growled
at him.

"I didn't see the gun. Besides, you should have stayed
inside." Right away Tony hated this man. If he hadn't been
in the way, he could have made the arrest.

"We had them right in our hands," Chad said, his face
scrunched up in pain. "All you had to do was stop them."

"Well, I tried, and you got in the way," Tony stammered.
"But I got their plate," he said, patting his pocket where
the card was stored safely with the numbers scrawled
across the top. "And believe me, I could positively identify
at least the bastard with the gun. Maybe all of them." The

whirl of the red light on top of the ambulance was giving him a headache.

"You're going to pay for this fuckup," Chad muttered, breathing heavily.

"Hey, I said I was sorry," Tony protested, his heart racing, suddenly aware that he was sweating. "I know my job and I did the right thing."

Thank God no one noticed that I dropped my gun.

"Never mind," Chad told him. "I'll call your chief later." Groaning, he flopped back on the gurney, whereupon the double doors slammed shut and the ambulance pulled away.

* * *

Maybe the Gordon's manager was pissed, but back at the station, Tony found that he had become a hero. When he walked in, everyone was bunched together as though posing for a picture, whistling and clapping madly. Loyal, goofy Bernie Pigeon jumped out of the group, shook a Sprite real hard and pointed it at Tony. "Way to go, buddy."

Later, Chief Fortini smiled at Tony across his desk. "Glad you're okay, boy. You really surprised me and I'm proud of the way you followed protocol. Your father and I handed this case to you on a silver platter, and you almost got the perps."

Not having missed Dan's word "almost," Tony pulled out the card with the license numbers on it and slapped it down in the middle of Dan's desk. "I got everything we need, Chief. The car was a full-sized, dark gray Pontiac with a New York license plate. We'll make a composite and blend it with the one from Parkdale. It should be a piece of cake to pick up those slime bags. Gimme Bernie, Chief, and we'll close the case in less than a week. I promise."

Dan leaned far back in his chair, the eraser end of a yellow pencil pressed against his lower teeth. "I don't know. I just don't know," he said, shaking his head. Tony had a sinking feeling. This was a giant step toward being a detective and he didn't want to blow it.

"Come on, Chief," Tony begged him. "Gimme a chance."

"Well," Dan said, clearly reluctant. "Okay, I guess. I could have Manfield handle all the North End beat while you're working on this. I've already sent out an all-points bulletin. So, all right, and yes, Bernie can assist. That's all you're going to get, though—one week. And you'd better come through this time."

The chief looked like he was already regretting his decision. Tony watched Dan's mouth pucker as he reached for the bottle of Tums in the top drawer of his desk.

Tony took a deep breath. "You can count on me, Chief," he said. "Absolutely. Positively."

And he meant it. To fail was not an option now.

"Not so fast, buster," Dan warned him. "You came damn near to screwing up today. What actually came down goes on file."

"Yeah, Chief, I know," Tony said, standing with his legs planted apart as though waiting to be slugged. "But, listen, His Honor won't necessarily have to see it, will he?"

Tony left without an answer because he knew what it would be. His Honor always found out. All his life, Tony had never gotten away with anything.

But things are going to change, starting now.

* * *

CHAPTER EIGHT

"What's weighing down that BB brain of yours?" Tony said, looking across the desk at Bernie.

"Well, New York called."

Tony leaned forward. "And?"

"They ran the license number you gave them to a white Chevrolet and found that the plates had been turned in and not reissued." Bernie was facing away from Tony, talking to the wall. It was really annoying. But Tony also knew that it was his way of softening lousy information.

"Did you tell the assholes to keep looking?"

"Yeah. I even suggested they change the V to a U and try again and that check led them to a dark blue, full-sized car owned by a black man by the name of Casey who lives in Harlem," Bernie continued in a monotone that was even more annoying than his staring at the wall. Tony felt a gas pain working its way into his lower bowel.

"You must've got some of the numbers wrong."

"No, shithead, I didn't get anything wrong."

"In any case—"

"In any case, what? You weren't there." In the middle of Tony's desk was an 8x10 paper with 2634WMV written at the top. Choosing a black felt-tipped pen, he traced each number and letter making them wider and darker. It had to be right. He had been so sure.

Tony looked at the man who had been his friend since they both had been in diapers and shrugged. "So what am I," he demanded, "Mister Perfect? Christ, Bernie, *they were shooting at me*. I did well to get as much info as I did without getting myself killed. Those guys in New York may consider this a dead end, but I'm going to bust this investigation wide open."

Tony walked over to the coke machine and dropped in some coins. When nothing happened, he smacked it with the butt of his hand and a can dropped down the chute to the tray below. Picking up the ice-cold can, he pressed it to his forehead.

"Hey, the last time I saw you get so worked up was when you lost that fourteen-inch trout," Bernie said, changing the subject again, playing Mr. Psychology. "Or maybe it was over Debbie Ann last Saturday night."

"Screw that, Bernie," Tony protested. "We've gotta put our heads together. This is our future we're discussing here." He tore Monday off of the calendar, balled it, and threw it in the wastebasket. "We've got the law on our side and a couple of good brains," he added. Glancing down at his notes, he saw that he had drawn a line through the numbers. When did he do that?

"Gee, thanks for the compliment, buddy."

Tony picked up the phone on the second ring.

"I'm calling from Dalton, Connecticut," a police officer told him. "Since you guys are taking the lead in this Gordon's case, we thought you'd want to know that two men and a woman were observed hanging around the jewelry counter at the Gordon's here in Dalton. They later split up outside the store. The license number of one of the men was recorded, and we stopped him out on Route 8 where our guys found a guy by the name of Ivan Petroff behind the wheel."

"Did they arrest him?" Tony demanded, signaling Bernie to pick up the extension.

"No, given the fact that there was insufficient cause, they couldn't do that. But they did get his address and the place where he worked."

"Fantastic." Tony looked across their desk to be sure Bernie was writing all the important stuff down. "This is just the lead we're looking for. Thanks. We owe you."

"This is it, Bernie-boy," he exclaimed, jumping to his feet, energized. "Let's grab that composite from Parkdale and haul ass for Dalton."

"Shouldn't we wait for the composites from that guy Richardson?" Bernie asked as they hurried toward their cruiser.

"Nah, this one's enough. Besides, I know what they look like, for crissakes. I wanna move on this fast. Both the chief *and* the mayor have my tail in a vice. We can catch something to eat on the way."

Tony could tell by the look on Bernie's face that he disapproved of his suggestion. One of the things that irritated him about Bernie was his lack of interest in food. And that wasn't all. Bernie must think he was an ass kisser, and maybe he was. Sometimes. But what's the need of kissing ass when you know all the right people?

Taking advantage of his flashing lights, they sped down the interstate with Tony at the wheel, watching speeders hit their brakes when they approached. Everyone's got a guilty conscience.

It was mid afternoon, the velvet hour. At the point of farthest visibility, the air was silver and slate, darkening near the horizon, almost purple. Something was building out there. New weather perhaps, or new opportunity. *New me*, Tony told himself.

* * *

By the time they got to the Dalton police station, Ivan Petroff had been eliminated as a suspect because the modus operandi didn't match at all, not to mention the fact that he had had such a heavy accent that he could barely speak understandable English. Besides, who would cash a check and show his driver's license if he was robbing the place? But, undaunted by the information, Tony insisted on interrogating Petroff at his place of work. At the academy, he had been taught never to ignore a coincidence or a hunch.

The minute Petroff entered the room, Tony knew he wasn't their man, but he showed him the composite anyway. The guy was scared, that was obvious—probably thinking of the KGB. If he knew anything, Tony'd bet his ass he'd tell.

"Zat man looks ze same as ze vun who yust moved in upstairs," he stated almost immediately. "And *she* looks like ze landlady," he added, pointing at the female accomplice, following which he raised both hands in the air as if having been asked to surrender.

"What now?" Bernie asked after they thanked Petroff and returned to the cruiser.

"We're here, so we might as well check out his testimony," Tony said, absently running his finger inside his shirt collar. Too much friggin' starch.

"It's a pretty flimsy lead."

"I don't need you to tell me that."

That was the trouble with him, Tony thought, as they pulled out of the parking lot and headed for 19 Hedgerow Drive in Dalton where Mr. Petroff lived. Bernie had this thing about proof. Sometimes it drove Tony crazy. On the other hand, he depended on Bernie's cautiousness to rein in his impulsive nature. Bernie had always done that for him.

✳ ✳ ✳

CHAPTER NINE

Eric Nordblum was startled when the doorbell rang. Could it be Shelly? She was the only one who knew exactly where he was living. A little flutter of hope rose in his chest. He never had visitors and, for that matter, could not remember ever having heard the bell ring before. And it was being rung with an unpleasant insistence, over and over again.

"Hello, may I help you?" Eric asked, releasing the chain lock, surprised to see two New Jersey cops standing in the hallway. His heart sank. Could this be about divorce papers? From the open door, a cold blast of air ripped through the room.

"We could use your help, sir," the stocky fellow said and then he stopped just inside the door and stared at Eric as though he was trying to place him and not doing a very good job of it.

"Have you ever seen me before?" The cop's question came out of nowhere.

"No. Never. Why?"

"We're police detectives," he said, ignoring Eric's question. "Get out your badge, Bernie. By the way, my name is Tony Deluca. Detective Deluca and this is Detective Bernard Pigeon. And your name is?"

Eric told them his name. Anxious about what the heck detectives wanted with him, he stepped back into the apartment, allowing them to pass through the narrow entryway.

"Has something happened to my boys?"

"No, that isn't it, we'd just like to chat a bit about a situation," Tony told him.

"What kind of situation?" Eric said. Maybe Shelly was having him followed. If that was the case, they could damn well report that he was living like a monk here. But if they were spying on him, they wouldn't have revealed themselves.

"Well, it seems that some questions have come up about a case of identification," Tony said. "Mind if we sit? It's been kind of a long day."

"Go ahead," Eric said, grabbing a vinyl chair for himself from the kitchen. He couldn't imagine why he would feel embarrassed about this pitiful excuse for a residence in front of people he didn't even know, but he did. The one called Tony sat on the lumpy couch and the other one started looking around the room. *He better not touch any of my papers. And if they're working for Shelly, I'd better watch what I say.*

"Okay, here's the deal," Tony said, taking the lead. Flashing the composite picture under Eric's nose, he then dropped it on the coffee table. "It seems that your friend, Mr. Petroff, thought this sketch looks a little like someone in this building," Tony told him. "Maybe a little like you."

He was bewildered and dismayed. "I don't look anything like him," Eric protested. "Can't you see that?"

"Sure. But do you know who this guy might be? Maybe he lives upstairs or visits someone who lives here? Anyways, it's someone who travels a lot."

"Whoa," Eric broke in with a nervous laugh. "That's a lot of questions. Slow down and give me a chance to think. First of all, Mr. Petroff's not my friend. I've only passed him in the entry a few times. Let me look at that picture up close."

He carried it over to his desk where he held it under the light. *This is absurd, them asking me to identify some criminal.* At least he assumed that this was what their visit was about.

"Nope, it's definitely not me and I've never seen anyone who looks like him," he told them, handing it back to Bernie. He remained standing, hoping they'd get the hint.

"Does he travel?" Tony insisted.

"Does who travel?"

"The guy upstairs."

"I don't know," Eric told them, impatient now. "I have no idea what he does. Furthermore, I've never seen him in a car. I only live here occasionally."

Again, Tony was holding the sketch up, looking from it to Eric as though he expected either one to morph into an exact likeness.

"So, you drive around a lot, like back and forth for business?" he asked. "What do you get around in?"

"What do you mean?"

"What kind of car do you drive?" Bernie spoke slowly as if addressing a child.

"A Pontiac. You must have seen it outside."

"What color is it?" Tony said, inching forward on the couch.

"It's two-toned gray," Eric told them. *Now what the hell had he said to make these guys exchange a significant look?*

"So that's *your* car in the driveway?"

Eric went over to the window. *Why were they so interested in his car? They can see for themselves it hasn't been in an accident.* He didn't like the way things were going here.

"We noticed that the antenna was bent. Now, can you tell us just how that happened?"

"Easy. It got bent at Eastman's Car Wash over on Turner Street, right here in town." This questioning didn't make any sense.

Eric saw Tony raise his eyebrows at Bernie as if what he had said was significant.

"We were just wondering," Bernie said, at which point he leaned toward Tony and whispered something before pulling a card out of his wallet and beginning to read the familiar Miranda warning. "Eric Nordblum, you have the right to remain silent . . ."

"What the hell . . . what are you charging me with?" Eric said, clearing his throat and plunging both hands deep in his pockets. This sounded like serious trouble. He'd better keep his head or things would get out of control.

"It's just a formality whenever we talk to someone," Tony said, while the thin detective beside him nodded in agreement. "Does it bother you?"

"I haven't done anything wrong," Eric said wearily. "I'm not involved in anything. Go ahead, but I want to wrap this up. I have business calls to make before six." *This is a bunch of doubletalk. I don't think Shelly would have anything to do with these clowns, so why are they talking to me?*

As Tony continued his barrage of questions, Bernie began wandering around the room, picking up things and setting them back down, not necessarily where they had been. "What's your line of business, uhh, Eric?" he said when Tony paused for breath. "You don't mind if we call you Eric, do you?"

"It's okay, I guess," Eric told him, glad for a break in the rapid questioning. "Actually, I'm a sales engineer."

Why he was even answering their questions was beyond him. What he did was none of their damn business. He was getting seriously pissed.

"Keeps me on the go a lot," Eric added, his voice faltering as he glanced over at the photos of his sons.

"Live here alone, Eric?" Tony asked. "Out on the road most of the time, you say? What about family, girlfriends? You know, things like that?"

"You have to be kidding. I'm a married man." Now they were going to ask about Shelly and he didn't want her to come into the conversation. Also, for some reason, he really resented being called by his first name. "I travel back and forth throughout the Northeast. That's my territory."

Things were definitely off-kilter here. They suspected him of something, but what? The apartment was getting stuffy. Eric thought he could smell his own sweat. To think he had been cold in this stinking place just before they showed up.

"I demand to know why you're here!" he said belligerently, because that's how he felt. "What do you think I'm involved in, for God's sake?"

"We're about done here," Tony said to his sidekick. "We need to head back to Radcliff. How often do you go through there?" he asked, quickly turning back to Eric.

"Where?"

"New Jersey."

"Often," Eric told him. "My kids are in Tolleson and it's part of my territory as well. This apartment is just a temporary place because I travel a lot. Look, I want to know what this is all about. I could be more helpful if I knew what you're after."

"Well, we're investigating some robberies that occurred in the past few weeks," Bernie told him affably.

Even though a robbery had absolutely nothing to do with him or Shelly, Eric was beginning to suspect that these guys still might have a reason to be questioning him. They were starting to scare him again. Particularly the one called Tony who looked as though he really had an agenda.

"Ever been in Parkdale or Lewisburg?" Tony interrupted, "How about Radcliff?

"Sure, I told you I've been all around the Northeast."

"Ever been in a Gordon's? Pick up something for the girlfriend?"

"I don't have a girlfriend." Eric heard his voice rising again.

"Do you own gold cuff links with diamonds on them?"

"I don't wear jewelry." And then, glancing down at his hand, "well, just a wedding band."

"Ever do drugs?" Tony fired at Eric. His flip tone was like sandpaper.

"Of course not! Why would you ask?"

"How about women? A good-looking blonde?" Tony suggested. "Casual dates, stuff like that. How many pads like this one do you have?"

Seeing the suspicious look in Tony's eyes as he looked quizzically around the shabby room, it occurred to Eric that he might think this was some kind of criminal hideaway.

"Stop," Eric said, trying not to raise his voice. "I said I'm married and this isn't a pad. Look, I'd really like to help you on this investigation, but I've told you, I don't know anything about the guy upstairs. Why don't you go up and ask him yourselves?"

The minute he said it, Eric realized that he might have gone too far. They might be obnoxious, but they were *detectives* and they seemed determined to catch him in some kind of a lie. Agitated, he began to pace. He desperately wanted them to leave.

"I'm not a suspect in something, am I?" he asked. "Look, I keep a DayTimer," he told them, not waiting for an answer. "It's a pocket-sized record book, sort of a diary, telling where I've been and what I did. I also have an answering service. In fact, I'll go get my DayTimer for you right now, and this whole business can be put to rest. See? Here it is. Okay. When and where did this thing happen? I can prove where I was any day of the week, including weekends."

"Calm down," Tony told him, getting to his feet. "A calendar of your activities wouldn't be considered proof of anything and a diary is such a personal thing that it couldn't be counted as an alibi in the real sense of the word. But, hey, listen, we really do appreciate your being cooperative and all. Hell, sometimes people clam right up and won't say a word to us. It's so much easier when they do. What's your address in Tolleson and maybe we should have your Social Security number, too. Would you take those down, Bernie?"

Eric gave him a long narrow look. "Why would you need that information?"

"Just to make our report complete. We have to keep track of whoever we talk to, you know," Tony said.

"We can always get this information on our own," Bernie chimed in. It was an unmistakable threat.

"Well, it sure seems odd," Eric said, reluctantly fishing his wallet out of his pocket. "All right, is there anything else before you leave?"

As he ushered them toward the door, he found himself wishing he could kick their butts down the stairs.

"Geez, you have really been a great help, Eric," Tony told him, suddenly holding up an old Polaroid camera which Eric hadn't noticed until now. "And hey, look, for the sake of the record and all, how about if we snap a photo of you to clip to the report? It'll help us remember who we interviewed on this damn case and put a face with the words. We talk to so many people, it can get confusing."

Eric blinked at the flash. The important thing was for him to get these skunks out the door. It seemed as though he was losing control of everything in his life. The thought made him feel sick in the pit of his stomach.

He watched as they clumped down the stairs. *My God, I don't know exactly what they suspect me of—who's more of a moron, them or me?*

✳ ✳ ✳

CHAPTER TEN

When they reached the driveway, Tony walked over to Eric's Pontiac and told Bernie to get a shot of the car. "And be sure to include the antenna," he added. "Take it from this side."

Here he was, face-to-face with both the shooter and the getaway car, and yet, *and yet*, not everything lined up. Before all this happened, he might have looked at the evidence differently, but Dan was depending on him, and nailing someone in one week would certainly get Pop's attention. Maybe not his love, but certainly his respect. Eric looked a little older than the shooter, but then, it was the end of the day and he had more than a five o'clock shadow. And the guy was scared. That was obvious and anyone who is scared usually has something to hide. Tony knew all he had to do was set things in motion. He wouldn't be actually fingering the guy, just bringing him into focus.

Once they were safely in the cruiser and well out of earshot, Bernie said, "Christ, can you imagine, he even let us take his picture. And he was smiling the whole time. For someone who had the finger pointing at him, he was damn cooperative."

"Yeah," Tony agreed, pulling out into the street. "Never mind the picture; can you believe we found this guy? We're geniuses. See, I told you we were right to talk to Petroff.

It was a gut feeling I had about this whole deal. Like His Honor says: *something smelled in Denmark*. And of course you know what clinched it, don't you, Bernie? The car. The goddamn gray Pontiac with the bent antenna sitting right there in the driveway—like it was waving a flag at us."

Even the car didn't *exactly* match his memory, but hell, how could anyone remember every little detail when they're being shot at? There's too much evidence here to be considered a coincidence.

"Maybe we should go back and pop a photo of the license plate, too," Bernie suggested.

"Nah, we don't need it now. I mean, the guy admitted that the car is his and as far as the plate is concerned, obviously he would have changed it by now. At some point, we'll have to bring the car in as evidence, anyway. This guy has no idea what he's in for. No clue whatsoever. I'm sure I recognized him." Tony pushed down on the gas pedal. "We've got our man."

"Yeah," Bernie agreed as he socked his right fist into the palm of his other hand, "we've nailed the sonofabitch; ID, picture, and all. Where the hell did you pick up that interrogation spiel? From TV? You were good, Tony, real good. We make a great team."

"The first thing we gotta do with that picture is prepare a photo lineup," Tony told him. "We'll choose ten white suspects and feature our Mr. Nordblum's kisser front 'n center."

"But, a Polaroid shot in the center couldn't be any more suggestive if we ran neon lights around it."

"That's the whole idea, Sherlock. When you have evidence on your side, sometimes you have to push the envelope to get where you want to go. Remember what they said at the academy: 'amateurs practice until they get it right, professionals practice until they cannot get it wrong.'"

It was all too good to be true. They had somehow stumbled onto Eric, and Tony *knew* he was the one. Guilty as sin. *If not guilty, at least suspicious enough to be a serious suspect.*

"Did you take any notes?" he asked Bernie.

"Just a few."

"Not to worry," Tony replied nonchalantly. "We'll catch them up at some point."

"We were too busy interrogating the guy for me to write things down, remember? And let me tell you, I was observing his place. What a dump. He obviously needs the money from those diamonds."

"Or drugs."

"Yeah, or drugs."

"Hell, notes don't matter. We'll write up a report tying it all together first thing in the morning. Won't His Honor be proud and pleased?"

Tony picked up the cell phone and started to dial his father's number, but, on second thought, stopped and dropped it in the console between them, the dial tone vibrating accusingly. He'd better not jump the gun on this; Pop didn't like sloppy work.

"Yeah, yeah, he'll be proud of you, too, dummy, don't worry," Tony told him, aware in the darkness that Bernie had turned toward him. "If I get to continue as a detective, I'll request you as my permanent assistant."

"Great," Bernie said. He slumped down in his seat and closed his eyes. He was supposed to wear glasses to correct his lazy eye, but often he forgot to grab them when he left for work. "We'll be just like His Honor and the Chief," he muttered contentedly. "We'll have Radcliff in the palm of our hands."

* * *

After pouring himself a glass of wine, Eric dropped onto the threadbare couch, knowing there was more work to be done before he could sleep. He picked up a family photo that had been taken last Christmas and sighed. What a fool he had been. Look what he had thrown away. He wished he could turn the clock back to when he first met Shelly in Hoboken. Occasionally on a Saturday night they had splurged at Arthur's Tavern by ordering a pitcher of beer between them and talking to the bartender. What was his name . . .? Don something? Before the kids, before his big deal job, before taking their life together for granted— everything had been so simple then.

Those frigging detectives. How could any investigation have led them back to him in this rooming house—and especially through Petroff who could barely speak English? Eric wished he had asked more questions. Maybe he should call the police station to find out if they were legitimate. But then, he didn't want to draw attention to himself. Besides, he couldn't imagine that anything he had said to them had been helpful.

When Eric called home that evening to talk to Arthur and Jason, as he had almost every night since he left, he told Shelly about the menacing interrogation by the two detectives. For the first time since she had asked him to leave, he heard her laugh.

"I can't believe that, after nearly an hour of listening to that nonsense, you came away without knowing exactly what they thought you did," she said. "Honestly Eric, you'll always be the absent-minded professor. And they weren't even impressed with your government security clearance."

Actually, he couldn't recall if he had mentioned that or not, but then, it was all pretty much a blur now. The important thing was, for a moment, she had sounded like the old Shelly. He yearned to be there, to be in the place where his life made sense, to draw her against his chest, feel her heartbeat, her compliance. Was it, he wondered, possible that she was reconsidering his exile? It's always the same dream.

With another, deeper sigh, Eric reached for his DayTimer in which he faithfully entered his activities for the day. At the bottom of the page, he added: *Interrogated by a couple of jerks sent by the KGB.*

* * *

CHAPTER ELEVEN

Tony lay in his rumpled bed. It was part of the same maple set with matching bureau and mirror he had had as a boy. As soon as he had moved out, anything of his had been relegated to the basement of his father's house, where he even found the original brown and beige bedspread and his pine school desk and straight-back chair. For every time he had fallen in love in high school, he'd engraved a new heart on the top of the desk with the lucky girl's name in the center.

One thing he really enjoyed about his apartment was that it had a great view of the fireworks every Fourth of July and, just this week, almost everybody, including his landlord, had put their Christmas lights up. Holidays were especially lonely. Actually, they sucked, since Pop, who was the only family he had, chose to spend them with Shirley. Even volunteering to play Santa at the Senior Center last year hadn't impressed him enough to attend. The mayor, who always showed up at fundraisers and teas, couldn't be counted on when his son was doing something decent.

The place was a mess and he knew his mom would have disapproved—after all, he was twenty-four. If only she were still living, he wouldn't have been shoved out the door. He might as well have been an orphan at sixteen. Uterine cancer. It had all happened so fast.

Bernie still lived at home, the lucky stiff.

Tony bounded out of bed, eager to get to the station and see if there were any responses to the photo lineup that Bernie had circulated throughout the region. On their way back from Dalton, they had both been on a high, figuring they could be close to an arrest.

The pile of clothes ready for the Laundromat was growing. No wonder he couldn't hang on to a girlfriend for long. Eventually, they all wanted to get domestic. Either that or they looked at the way he lived and found it not very promising in terms of the long run. At least, that's what he told himself, although actually he knew his failed relationships were strictly his doing. If women got too close, he pulled back—afraid to commit. If Pop couldn't find something lovable in him—something to respect or be proud of—then who could? But, on the surface, he was still a lover-boy. Tony put his fingers to his lips and then on the photo of his mother that was wedged in the frame of the mirror and said, *"Morning, Mom."*

He peered at his reflection with a sense of satisfaction. After all, he was a very eligible bachelor. And soon they'd be able to read about him in the news.

Yeah, read it and weep, ladies.

* * *

At the station, the calls had already started coming in. The one that caught Tony's attention first off was from a detective by the name of Popoulas from Sutton, Connecticut. When Tony returned his call, Popoulas said that a single man had walked into their Gordon's, asked to see a bunch of rings, scooped them up, and run out of the store.

"That could be connected to our crime," Tony told him, elated.

Bernie, who was listening, whipped his head around to look at Tony in dismay when, in response to Popoulas saying that his suspect had a mustache, Tony suggested that Nordblum might wear a *false* one as part of a disguise.

Bernie quickly scribbled a note and flapped it in front of Tony's face: "*What kind of bullshit fairy tale are you telling this guy?*"

Tony waved it away and pushed his swivel chair around so his back was to Bernie and watched a huge spider making its way across a single thread of web strung from the corner of the window to the top of a city map pinned to the divider wall. It swayed precariously.

When the conversation came around to their suspect's motive for the theft, Tony told Popoulas that, judging from the apartment the suspect was living in, the guy obviously needed money. "His gray Pontiac was absolutely the getaway car," Tony told him. "I should know, I had my hand right on it as they drove away. I'm convinced that this guy Nordblum was the driver *and* the shooter."

"What the hell are you bugging me for?" Tony yelled at Bernie as soon as the call was over. "I was just baiting him, just trying to get as much info out of him as I could. I didn't even mention the Pontiac until he was done talking."

"But the problem is what you *implied*."

Tony felt a sudden surge of weariness. He wasn't *that* sure anymore. He needed to take that fact out and look at it because it was there like a stone. Where had he come up with the mustache? He wished he could pull back, but he knew that that was no longer an option. But Nordblum's car *is* gray, and *does* have a bent antenna. And his job takes him all around New England. Those are facts, ones that can be proven.

"Obviously, we need to persuade other police departments to jump on the bandwagon and back up an arrest," Tony explained slowly. "He's the one who had the gun. He's the one who drove the car. He could have killed me. Nordblum is our man and don't forget, nailing him will lead to detective status for both of us."

"Did Popoulas say if his witnesses mentioned anything about this guy missing some teeth?" Bernie asked.

"What the hell are you talking about, Bernie?"

"Remember when the witness from Parkdale, what's-her-name, Mary something, said that one of the robbers was missing some teeth?"

"Yeah, I remember, the salesgirl from Parkdale. But what am I supposed to do, look in everybody's stinkin' mouth? Jesus, Bernie, you have some of the worst ideas."

* * *

Within minutes, Tony was in the driver's seat of the squad car, yelling to Bernie to hurry up and join him. When he was halfway in, Tony squealed into such a sharp U-turn that Bernie's door swung shut on his leg.

"For crissake, what the hell is your rush?" he demanded. "I almost lost my leg."

"Buckle up, sissy," Tony told him, "don't forget, Chief gave us one week, one friggin' week to make an arrest. We're going to take our lineup photo over to Gordon's now and flash it at the salespeople. See what they say. Check their reactions. I'll do the talking; you just listen and observe, and if anyone says something important, write it down this time."

"What do you mean, 'this time'? You didn't tell me to write anything before."

"Forget it, I'm not blaming you, but we've gotta get caught up on that shit."

When they walked into the store, Tony deliberately passed the manager's office, walking straight to the fine jewelry section. *I'm not showing this lineup to that bastard Richardson who blames me for his bum leg and for those dickheads getting away. Screw him.* Tony wasn't going to give Richardson the opportunity to contradict him or screw up his memory of what happened.

The woman at the jewelry counter picked out Eric's picture on the grounds that it looked *the most like* the guy who had come into the store that day. More, at least, she had added, than that first composite. Her sales associate picked out Eric's picture after she saw who her boss had chosen, saying that she *believed* it was him although she wasn't sure enough to make a positive identification.

"Shit! That was a bust," Bernie said, once they were back in the car. "Those knuckleheads were unable to make a positive ID."

"Or unwilling."

"You think they were holding back on us?"

Tony didn't answer. He decided to dump Bernie off at the station while he followed up on the New York investigation where another lead had come in. Tony didn't want him monitoring every damn word he said.

"While I'm gone, you send out more lineup shots and don't volunteer anything to the chief. If he asks how the investigation is going, just tell him I'll have it wrapped up before the end of the week, just as I promised."

"You mean, *we*, don't you, Tony, *we'll* wrap it up?" Bernie asked, tipping his head to the side and raising his eyebrow.

Tony felt something in the air, something not quite like a threat, more like a simmering resentment that could turn back into respect at any time. "Yeah, okay, you can say we," Tony replied without looking at him.

"All right buddy, I'll stick to the grunt work here while you do the fun part," Bernie said, punching Tony in the shoulder, slightly harder than was strictly necessary as he got out of the car. He grinned when Tony cringed at his touch.

Although he loved Bernie like a brother, Tony needed to be the hero in this case. That would be talking Pop's language. There was room for only one man to get the vote, one man to catch the criminal.

* * *

After dropping Bernie at the station, Tony took a quick detour over to his father's office.

Shirley was decorating a Christmas tree in the reception room with the same stuff that his mother used to decorate Pop's office with each year. *There's the angel I made in fourth grade. Can't believe that's still around.*

"Hi, Shirley. Is His Honor in?" he said loudly enough so that his father would hear him.

"Come on in here, boy," Angelo Deluca called from behind his massive desk, his tremendous girth completely enveloping the chair beneath him. He didn't attempt to rise from it to greet Tony.

"What're you here for? You're supposed to be working," Angelo said as he flipped through papers in front of him.

"I know, but I just stopped by to tell you I've got that Gordon's case under wraps. I'll probably be bringing in the main suspect by the end of the week . . . just before Christmas."

"Yeah, that would be good, especially after the way you almost screwed up the sting," Angelo replied. *There was that 'almost' word again. Like a threat.*

Shifting his weight to lean forward over his desk, his dark eyes nearly buried in loose flesh, Angelo looked at his son with the expression that Tony knew only too well. "So how come you haven't been over to your mother's grave?"

"I have Pop, but this week I've been busy trying to bust this case."

"Don't call me Pop in my office, dammit. When I'm here, I'm *His Honor.* That's for you and everyone else."

"Okay, His Honor. So, I'll see you later."

Tony turned on his heel and left the office. On his way through the reception area, he yanked the stupid angel off the tree and stuffed it in his pocket. His father's voice followed him as he hurried down the long dark corridor to the elevator, "Remember that I come up for a new term next year," he heard his father shout, "and I don't need any mess stirred up by you sitting on my back. Get those guys and bring them in. No matter what."

Just because someone thinks you are shit sometimes, doesn't mean you always are, Tony told himself. But that didn't make him feel any less afraid. What did he mean by "no matter what?" Was that a message? Or some kind of a green light?

* * *

Tony drove over to New York on Route 287 as far as the Dunkin' at Exit 5, maintaining a steady speed of eighty, with the result that he arrived in Kensington in half the time it should have taken. He felt as though he was racing from here to there almost randomly, but he knew if the week ended and he didn't have the suspects, or at least one, behind bars, Dan would replace him with a more experienced detective. Then, who knew how long it would be before another chance to impress His Honor would come up?

Over coffee, he exchanged information with Detective Fornier whose first question was, "How the hell did those bastards get away with the ring?" to which Tony replied that he could have been killed when they shot at him and that the manager panicked and got in the way.

"Now tell me how you ever found this guy Nordblum in the first place?"

"Good detective work." Tony flashed a tentative smile. "His car is a perfect match, right down to the bent antenna. It was sitting right there in plain sight. Besides, I'd know that face anywhere. And we might have a couple of positive witnesses right in Radcliff, too," Tony added, without exactly looking him in the eye when he said that.

On the way back to Radcliff, Tony left a message on Bernie's phone: "I'm running late, so I'll eat on the way and meet you at the Moonglow around eight," he said. "I'm hoping Debbie Ann will be there. And a babe for you, too, lover boy."

In the meantime, based on the information that Tony had given him, Detective Fornier had apparently driven right to his station with the photo lineup that had Eric's face staring out from exactly dead center.

* * *

When Tony and Bernie dragged into the station the next morning after a late night on the town, there was a message waiting for them from Fornier: "Good news, Detective Deluca," Tony read aloud. "We've got one positive witness for you."

Tony sat for a long time trying to think things through. Eric Nordblum was a scumbag, that was a given. If he weren't so absolutely sure that Nordblum was the shooter, he wouldn't even consider what he was thinking of doing. And then he wrote down *two* witnesses in Kensington.

* * *

CHAPTER TWELVE

Shelly rolled over in the king-size bed that she had shared with Eric for almost sixteen years. They had chosen the large size to accommodate Eric's height and his restlessness at night. Now she was lost in its emptiness.

She hadn't counted on the slowly mounting lure of their past. It seemed at once so near and so impossible, those years together. Memories rushed up, filling the room, holding her in place: Eric's touch, his pure joy of spending time with his sons, the way his hair drifted across his forehead when he was his most serious—how they would sit on the patio with a glass of wine, talking, planning, after the boys were in bed. Such simple things, really. Such tranquility.

She fingered the edge of the quilt her mother had made for them as a wedding gift. She had used a favorite dirndl skirt of Shelly's, working it into the pattern. Shelly's indecision wove its way through her yearning to go back to a place where her life had made sense. Going to the closet, smelling one of his shirts, she felt Eric's absence more than she had dreamed possible even though he had called faithfully every night to speak to the boys and hadn't missed one basketball game since he left home. She knew that he must have changed his schedule in order to make the games and how exhausted he must be with the extra commuting back and forth. He had pleaded with her to give him another chance, but so far, she hadn't given in.

She used to be the full-time librarian in Tolleson, but after the children arrived, Shelly had dropped back to working ten hours a week just to earn a little mad money and to keep her finger in the pie. Eric had told her many times that she should work only if she wanted to, that it wasn't necessary, never failing to assure her what a great mom she was. Now, since he had left, she had increased her hours and found to her surprise that she was enjoying it immensely. But with Christmas coming, she had begun to wonder if it was fair to keep Eric apart from the boys—*and from her, as well*—over the holidays.

She put on her robe and went down to the kitchen where she stopped in front of the coffee percolator. Since Eric had left, Shelly had had to struggle with the making of it—exactly how much per cup? Had he said that he added salt for extra flavor? Was it worth the trouble now, just for one person? Eric had been the one to start it brewing as soon as the alarm went off. She gazed out the window at how the snow crystals glistened on the bare limbs of the weeping cherry and how the lawns shimmered; luminescent as if under sea swells. Even though the boys helped, Eric had always done the lion's share of the shoveling. And the birdfeeders Eric had hung were empty. For a long time she sat still, agitated, on the edge of knowing what to do.

When Eric had called to tell her about that bizarre visit he had had by those crazy detectives from Radcliff, he had sounded so lonely that she had almost given in right then and told him to come home. Was he possibly in real trouble? Did he need her on a whole different level?

A ladybug coasted into the folds of the curtain and she remembered how, when they had rushed in through an open window each fall to the sanctuary of the heated room, Eric would lift them gently, place them on the leaf of a houseplant, and hope they would make it through the winter. Thoughts of his betrayal dropped like stones to the bottom of her consciousness and hid themselves between forgiveness and doubt. The separation hadn't accomplished what she had hoped, yet her sense of loss stirred up, like flames out of embers.

Don't give up, she heard a tiny voice whisper. *Your family's life will be better*. No further comment from the little voice about *her* life. What did it mean that lately she didn't see herself as the woman she remembered being before he left? No one could suspect the intricate mysteries of her dilemma, knowing clearly that you cannot go backwards in your life.

Suddenly the decision was hers, irrevocable, searing, and she made her choice partly because it was what she wanted, and partly for the boys who hadn't seemed the same since their father moved out.

Before she changed her mind, Shelly found herself picking up the phone and dialing Eric's number in Dalton, even though it was after ten. He answered with the first ring.

"Eric, we want you to come home," was all she said.

He drew in a sob, and then choked out: "All three of you?"

"Yes."

"I'll be there in two hours."

"You can wait till morning . . ."

"I'm coming now," he told her.

✵ ✵ ✵

CHAPTER THIRTEEN

Chief Fortini told Tony first thing the next morning that he thought they had enough evidence to seek an arrest warrant. "You'd better get Bernie in here," Dan growled. "I want you both on board for this."

Reaching to a shelf behind his desk, Dan pulled out a thick book that was part of a set and blew dust off the top of it. "I'm going to read to you two about what an arrest warrant involves," he told them. "You both pay attention. I'm quoting now. 'A judge must review the facts as presented by the officer who prepares an affidavit, sworn under the penalties of perjury, in which he lays forth facts and information allowing the judge to make an independent judgment as to whether or not he believes a crime has occurred and that the defendant committed the crime.'"

"That's what the Fourth Amendment in the Constitution is all about," Dan interjected, eyeing them sternly as if they hadn't been listening. "Without it, you have nothing." He closed the book with a clap. "Is that absolutely clear?"

"It sure is, Chief," Tony told him. "We're going to get right to it. Oh, and I'd like to remind you that it hasn't even been a week yet. Not bad for a couple of rookie detectives, huh, Chief?"

"You know what Yogi said; 'It ain't over till it's over'," Dan replied, "but, up to now, you're not doing too badly."

It was, Tony thought, a reluctant, back-handed compliment—but, he'd take it.

"Not to worry, Chief," he said, "and, hey, would you give His Honor a heads up for me?"

* * *

"Before we write up the affidavit, let's take a run over to Parkdale and interview that salesgirl," Tony said when they got back to their desks. "She's the one who got a really good look at them."

"Oh, so now you're a little nervous about your *two* positive witnesses?"

"Okay, so you want me to tell you I'm getting worried about witnesses?" Tony demanded. "Well, I am. You happy now?"

Jesus, he couldn't hide anything from Bernie. That's what comes with growing up together. "Quit looking at me like that," he went on. "Go get your glasses and grab the info on the witness. We gotta know who to talk to."

About an hour later, when Tony and Bernie approached Mary Fletcher's counter in cop uniforms, she hurriedly put away a tray of jewelry she had been arranging and stood, arms stiff at her sides, almost like she would salute any minute. That's a good attitude, Tony thought.

"Hi, how're you doing?" he said, smiling broadly.

"You're here about the ring robbery, aren't you?" she blurted out.

"Yeah, we're detectives from Radcliff. I'm Tony Deluca and he's Bernie Pigeon. We're here to show you a photo lineup. What we're looking for is a positive ID."

The guy she keeps glancing at must be her boss.

Bernie placed the lineup on the counter, facing it toward Mary, who stared at the pictures as though it were a tarantula. "Do you see anyone who resembles the man that robbed you?"

"Take your time," Tony said soothingly, glancing at Bernie over her bent head.

"I'm not sure . . . I don't know . . . I already told the Parkdale police everything." She clasped her arms tightly over her waist but it was evident that her hands were shaking. Tony could see clearly that they were going to have to push for a statement. If he couldn't get her to finger Nordblum, the entire case would slip through his fingers. And so would detective status, and so would praise from Pop.

"Did you know that the nice-looking man had a gun and shot at me?" he said, lowering his voice in order to sound as dramatic as possible, reaching out vocally to touch her conscience and her sympathy. "He almost killed the manager in another Gordon's. He's not what he looks like," he added, leaning intimately toward Mary. "We really need your help here, Miss Fletcher."

"Well, he did have dark hair, and looked about the same age . . ."

"Which one looks like that," Bernie asked impatiently, stabbing Eric's photo with his index finger, drawing Mary's attention right to it.

"That's the only one who resembles the younger thief," she said. Her words were tentative. "Is he the one who had the gun?" She sounded as though she could hardly comprehend it.

"Yes, and he's the one who shot at me," Tony told her again.

"It's a mystery to me," she said, shaking her head in disbelief. "He seemed so polite."

"Do you have a boyfriend, Miss Fletcher?" Tony asked. What was needed here was to make her comfortable, relaxed, and talking about something that makes her happy.

"Yes," she said, and now her voice was shrill. "Why do you ask? What does this have to do with him?"

Whoa. I hit a chord. I bet the boyfriend's been in trouble. Tony could tell that Bernie was thinking the same thing.

"There's no connection, believe me," he assured her. "I was just thinking that he'd want you to be safe."

"Could this man ever find out it was me if I identify him?"

"Absolutely not." Tony reassured her. He knew she was about to cave in. After all, he hadn't meant to pressure her. He was just trying to make her feel safe and comfortable enough to tell the truth. Actually, he pitied her. She seemed like a nice girl, probably a good Catholic, the kind of girl that his mom would have approved of. But he needed her confirmation. It would dispel twinges of doubt that had begun to torture him.

"You'd be protected by the law," Bernie echoed.

"Okay then, that's him." Suddenly her words were tumbling over one another as though some moral code had dissolved on her tongue, as though rushing this thing to a conclusion might make it go away. "The man in the middle. He is the one with the diamond cuff links, the one who acted so sophisticated."

Just then, her boss came over. "Can I help you fellas?" he said, his eyes narrowed. And when Mary explained falteringly that she had just identified the thief, he actually pushed her aside so he could scrutinize the photo lineup.

"Which one did you choose, Mary?" he asked without looking at her.

"The one in the middle." Now she was crying.

Without hesitation, her boss agreed.

Two positive IDs!

* * *

On the way back, Bernie fell asleep and Tony drove right past the Radcliff exit. Something was niggling at him even though he was relieved with Mary's ID. The friggin' antenna—that was it. Nordblum had to have made up that story. Nonetheless, he headed for that car wash in Dalton. The one that Eric had *claimed* had bent his antenna.

It's amazing how you can be so absolutely positive about something and then, as questions come up about it, the less certain you become. *I know I bent that damn thing and it was attached to a gray Pontiac,* he mumbled to himself as he turned off the highway. That's the line he had to take, and he had to stick with it.

* * *

A thick, well-muscled man in jeans and just a windbreaker stood like a guard in front of Eastman's Car Wash. The shadows were rapidly lengthening and the crisp air was filled with the metallic scent of winter.

"What are you, a lawyer, too?" he asked belligerently.

"No. I'm a detective," Tony told him, keeping his voice neutral.

"Well, you just look like a cop to me," the manager said.

"Don't be fooled by the uniform. How about answering my question."

"Look, we have a company policy; no antennas get broken in our car wash. Period. If we ever admitted to that, we'd be buying new ones for every Tom, Dick, and Harry. So there's no way I'm gonna say it happened here. Maybe it did and maybe it didn't. Either way, it's none of your business. It's between him and me. And I ain't budging."

Tony waved the lineup photo in front of the man a second time. "So you've never met the man in this picture?" He was desperate for a 'no' answer, but kept his tone under control.

"Yeah, I remember him complaining right after he went through the wash," the manager told him, pointing a stubby finger at the picture. "He seemed pretty honest and maybe I believed him, but there's no way in hell I'll ever admit to it. He could be trying to get me to pay for something that happened right in his own neighborhood, wherever the hell he's from. Maybe over Halloween."

"Does that mean you refuse to identify him?"

"Do you know how many people come through here in a day?"

"So what you're saying," Tony concluded, "is that his antenna did *not* get bent in this car wash, right?"

"Right. And this here conversation is over. I gotta get back to work."

* * *

"Where in friggin' hell have you been?" Bernie whined. "I'm sitting here without the keys, freezing my ass off with no idea why we're in Connecticut?"

"I was just checking out that car wash."

"Well?"

"He said it didn't happen there."

"You believe him?"

"Of course I believe him. What are you, stupid? I'm the one who bent the damn thing. So will you shut up and go back to sleep? I gotta think."

Bernie slumped down in the seat and jiggled his damn right foot halfway back to Radcliff.

Luck. Maybe that's all it was, Tony thought. That car wash guy will never acknowledge Nordblum's claim, so even if I am mistaken, which I'm sure I'm not, it'll never come out. Maybe the big things in life don't depend on how hard you try, how determined, how fair, how smart you are; maybe the whole shooting match depends merely on luck.

As he drove, he watched a pack of motorcycles slow down just behind his cruiser. He knew they didn't dare pass him. Tony pushed hard on the gas until they were out of sight.

Some things you want so badly you don't care how you get them. It doesn't matter if they're stolen or paid for because the trouble that may come later is of no consideration at the time. It scared him that he might end up behaving like his father; yet he wondered if, at some deep crazy level—was that what he actually hoped for?

✿ ✿ ✿

Tony sat in their cubicle with Bernie preparing the affidavit. They'd just finished describing the process by which they came to find Eric Nordblum as part of their investigation, how Ivan Petroff had fingered him. Tony stood looking over Bernie's shoulder as he painstakingly filled in the information to the effect that Nordblum had fabricated a story to explain the bent antenna.

It was, he thought, the first rung of the ladder of lies.

"And that there were two positive witnesses in New York that could identify Eric and two employees at the Parkdale Gordon's," Tony dictated. Bernie repeated the words as he wrote.

Bernie whispered, "Not without a little exaggeration and persuasion."

"You shut your mouth," Tony warned him, scowling. "They picked him out of eleven mug shots of guys that were similar in size, age, and characteristics—just what the book required. And when you finish this thing, we both gotta sign it. Right there where it says, 'Sign under penalty of perjury.'"

If he played everything strictly by the book, Nordblum could get away with the crime. And they had no other suspects.

Bernie stood and wandered over to the window and then to the water cooler. "We might just as well have shown that lineup photo at random to people on the street in Newark."

"Look at me, Bernie—do you or don't you want to be a detective?"

"You know that's what we've both wanted since we were kids."

"Okay. Then sign the friggin' thing and be done with it."

"Well, as Grandpa Pigeon used to say at his poker games: In for a penny, in for a pound. Give me the pen."

There was something eerie and frightening about actually signing the affidavit. Doubt ran through Tony's brain, barely discernable as independent thoughts. Perhaps it was naked fear, he thought, that becomes so profound that it would defeat anyone who tried to carry it alone.

* * *

CHAPTER FOURTEEN

Arriving home, Eric entered through the garage and tiptoed into the kitchen. He drew in a sudden breath when he saw what Shelly had left for him on the counter—his mother's coffee cake, loaded with extra cinnamon. *His favorite smell and taste.* Pulling out a stool, he sat up to the center island where he savored each bite, finding comfort in being surrounded by so much that was familiar—the boys' homework leaning against their lunch bags, *two* coffee cups next to the percolator, ready for the morning rush. Nearly overcome with a contentment he had almost forgotten, he pulled the family photos out of his suitcase, replacing them exactly where they had been that horrible night nearly a month ago. There was even a note from Jason and Arthur on the coffee table. *Welcome home, Dad.* She must have had to rouse them from sleep to tell them.

Uncertain as to where Shelly wanted him to sleep, he stood beside the couch for a moment, and then, slipping off his shoes, climbed the stairs to their bedroom. Although it was dark outside, when he entered their room, Eric could see clearly that Shelly was awake, reaching out to him with bare arms.

He was truly home at last.

✻ ✻ ✻

Eric, ecstatic to be back in Tolleson, wasn't taking anything for granted. Knowing that it would require more than wine and flowers to win back Shelly's trust, he was as attentive to her and to the boys as a man could be. With each new day, Eric felt that their relationship was becoming less fragile.

Tonight, he draped his arm across the back of the couch, gently caressing her slender neck. A pale slant of winter light, already fading, came in the south window, resting before them on the living room floor as they each enjoyed a glass of chardonnay.

So absorbed was he in his family that he had not given another thought to the detectives' visit at the apartment in Dalton until this evening when Shelly asked him if anything further had come of it.

"Maybe you should talk to someone about it," she suggested. "It makes me a little nervous."

Before leaving for work the next morning, Eric spoke to his brother-in-law who recommended an attorney who was a senior member of the bar from one of the large and prestigious law offices in Trenton. When Eric reached Attorney Delmar at his office, he seemed hard put to suppress his surprise as he listened to Eric describe the strange encounter he had had with the detectives who had come all the way from New Jersey to interview him in Connecticut. He agreed, however, to make a call to clear up the matter, although, as he told Eric, it looked to him to be an open-and-shut situation.

"If this turns out to be something real, I'll tell the Meriden county prosecutor that we'll be supplying irrefutable alibi evidence to her," he said. "What we would want is the opportunity to present your evidence at a Probable Cause Hearing. That's when it would end, Eric. At a Probable Cause Hearing. If," he added under his breath, "they don't indict you first."

"Okay," Eric said. He felt the tightness in his throat ease ever so slightly. He liked the fact that Delmar seemed to be a man of action. "How soon can we get that set up?"

"Everything in good time," the attorney assured him dismissively. "I'll keep you informed."

Eric could only hope that this was a trumped-up thing that would all go away with one phone call to the Radcliff prosecutor.

* * *

Tony stared at Judge Herman Barrington, a nondescript man made large by the weight of judicial power, and he waited. The judge's light brown hair was thin on top but he had combed the few sparse strands over to the other side. He raised his shaggy eyebrows at him. "Well?" his voice rose into a question.

Clearing his throat, Tony started to read from the affidavit in his hand. This was his first request for an arrest warrant.

The first of many, after he officially became Detective Deluca.

"No, no, no," Judge Barrington barked impatiently, reaching over the bench toward him. "Here, give me that paper. I don't like to be read to."

Settling back into his seat, he unfolded the glasses that hung from around his neck.

Tony looked over at Bernie with a nervous half-smile while Bernie took a deep breath and held it, focusing on the huge wall clock directly over the judge's head.

"You can attest to all of this?" the Judge asked, looking at both of them, holding Tony's paper in one hand and flicking it with the fingers of the other.

"Yes, sir," Tony replied, realizing that he actually felt a film forming over the truth, a barrier as brittle and fragile as ice, impenetrable, opaque. A landscape from which there was no return.

"And we know where Mr. Nordblum is living," Tony added. "The getaway car is actually sitting right in his driveway."

Show confidence, he told himself. We have to do whatever is needed to put this guy behind bars, *no matter what*.

Judge Barrington's eyelids looked lizard-like in their slowness; they closed once, and then twice, as if, Tony thought, to wash the glare of boredom from his eyeballs.

"Raise your right hands," he said, finally looking up from the affidavit: "Do you swear under penalty of perjury that this warrant is true and is based on your personal knowledge that a crime has been committed and that the defendant committed that crime?"

Tony stood tall, raised his right hand and said, "I do, Your Honor," looking Judge Barrington right in the eye, thankful that the judge couldn't hear the thump of his heart.

Bernie raised his right hand and mumbled something unintelligible, his lazy eye wandering farther than usual.

"Okay, boys, you've got it," the Judge said, as he signed a warrant for the arrest of Eric Nordblum for alleged Assault With a Deadly Weapon and First Degree Larceny at multiple Gordon's locations, most specifically Radcliff, New Jersey.

* * *

When Frank Delmar called Eric back, he felt like a shaft of ice had been plunged into his bloodstream. "*What?*" Eric hissed into the receiver, closing his office door to make sure that no one was listening, his thoughts skipping wildly from one dire possibility to another. "An arrest warrant? For what, for God's sake?"

"It seems that a number of people have identified you in these Gordon's robberies," Delmar told him. "Apparently there was a shooting involved, but no one was killed. I know you have an alibi, so it's just a formality, Eric, but I'm afraid that I have to accompany you to the Radcliff police station tomorrow morning. You'll need to bring your checkbook to pay a $2,500 retainer so that I will officially be your lawyer."

"No one was killed? Who was shot? Jesus, I've never owned a gun in my life."

"Nonetheless, you need to show up there voluntarily to be booked and then you can go back to work. If you don't go under your own steam, they will come to your workplace or home and formally arrest you."

He barely heard the rest of what the attorney said—something about the police coming to arrest him. Suddenly, everything about Eric's life seemed to have changed. He started to perspire and his face grew hot as he glanced at his co-workers through the glass door of his office. Jake Adams with that wimpy grin of his was talking to Maggie—acting like he owned the place. *He'd love to hear I'm in trouble.*

To obtain more details from his attorney was beyond Eric's emotional reach at the moment. "When and where?" he finally asked in an unsteady voice.

When Delmar told him he would pick him up the next morning at seven, Eric couldn't answer. He just hung up, feeling like he was standing in the path of a tsunami.

✻ ✻ ✻

CHAPTER FIFTEEN

In Sherman's Diner, Dan looked across the red Formica table at Angelo. Radcliff's home boys were sitting in front of the picture window reminiscing about past triumphs on the football field. "Someday we're really going to write that memoir," Angelo said for the umpteenth time, "our glory days—quarterback and fullback—still stars today."

Dan had maintained his slim wiry stature by virtue of sheer nervous energy and an unprecedented drive to succeed, which he knew bugged the shit out of Angelo who was too big now to squeeze into the booth where they had once held court in high school. Dan never had the charm or ability to persuade people to do things his way, like Angelo did, and that bugged the shit out of Dan. His friend was powerful, influential, and still handsome, in an enlarged sort of way. Furthermore, Angelo's family had a lot of money. As a matter of fact, the residents of Radcliff had recently voted to name the new bridge that had just been completed on the edge of town, the Deluca Bridge, in his honor.

No one was naming a bridge for him.

Dan had fought hard for every step he had taken up the ladder and he knew that, in the process, he had made enemies who were out there gunning for his position as

Radcliff's Police Chief. He saw lines across his cheeks and deep furrows between his eyes every morning when he shaved, signs that he had paid the price. Angelo was always joking that Dan's teachers probably would have deemed him hyperactive if someone had given that condition a name back when they were in grade school. But then again, Angelo would readily admit that Dan could make quick decisions, and was most always right.

They had just begun to discuss the Gordon's case when a man came into the diner and called over to their table. "Hey, guys," he said. "I hear young Tony cracked the shooting over at the mall."

Angelo smiled broadly. "Actually, Gordon's has stores all over the Northeast," he said, "so we're going to get a lot of publicity out of this. And that's a good thing."

Dan frowned. "Nothing's for sure till those bastards are behind bars, but it's looking good, Angelo . . . looking good. What I'm hoping now is that Nordblum will rat out his accomplices. I'm putting a tail on him in case they're in touch. Your boy may have crossed the line a bit on this thing," Dan said to Angelo, now lowering his voice, "but it does looks like he and Bernie have cornered Nordblum." He wanted to be certain that if there *had* been any crossing of the line, it wouldn't be attributed to him.

A committed bachelor, Dan had never been able to get a grip on father and son relationships, but he was well aware of the conflict between Angelo and Tony. Angelo had never made any bones about the fact that he couldn't accept his own son. As far as Dan was concerned, Tony would go right back to the beat as soon as there was an arrest. One thing for damn sure, he'd never measure up to Angelo.

Angelo concentrated on pushing the last bite of a chili meatball sandwich into his mouth and chewed thoughtfully for a while before speaking. "This is going to look real good for both of us next November," he said with an exaggerated wink, the kind he so often gave to the voters.

Dan felt an uneasiness that he couldn't quite identify. But he knew one thing for sure; it had to do with Tony. Tony and Bernie.

* * *

Shelly was just getting ready for work, when the phone rang in the kitchen. At first, she thought Eric was joking when he told her about the disastrous news. "What do you mean by an arrest warrant?" she said. "They've got to be kidding. The idea of you stealing something is positively absurd."

"Well, Delmar just called and he definitely was not joking, I can tell you that," Eric said emphatically. "He's picking me up at the house at seven tomorrow morning. So, we'll tell the kids he's a business associate. Okay?"

She could tell that Eric was clenching his teeth.

"Okay, Shelly? Okay?" he repeated.

"Tell me what I should do." The image of her husband standing alone and frightened in his office in Connecticut burned behind her eyelids.

"Keep your voice down," Eric warned her, dropping his own a few decibels. "Don't tell anyone."

He's forgotten that the boys are in school at this hour. Besides, who was she going to tell?

"Delmar said that after I show up at the police station, I have to go upstairs to the court to pay bail. Cash. Would you please get some money from the bank for me?"

"How much?"

"I don't have a clue . . . Five hundred? A thousand?"

"Where should I take it out of . . . the college account?" Shelly left the sentence in the air, as if she were afraid of finishing it or wasn't sure how to.

"Oh, good God. Yes, wherever." Eric's voice came out quavering, an alien sound that she heard with alarm.

"Then what will happen, Eric?"

"How the hell should I know?" All the caring he had shown her when he had returned home seemed to have disappeared. "This is my first arrest, in case you didn't realize it."

She wanted to sit down, but something stopped her. Instead, she leaned against the wall for support. *Why is he attacking me? The lawyer said it's just a formality. Sweet Jesus, this is becoming a nightmare.* And something told her it was going to get worse.

※ ※ ※

Somehow Eric got through the night. Not even pretending to sleep, he and Shelly lay side by side, silently listening to the wind as, relentless and wet, it ushered in winter with freezing temperatures and a few inches of snow. By six forty-five, haggard and tense, they were both pacing in front of the living room window, watching for the attorney. Good to his word, Frank pulled up right on time and Eric rushed out to the car, not even bothering to call goodbye to the boys who were still in their bedrooms upstairs. Nor did he look back at Shelly. He prayed that no neighbors were watching.

Before putting on his seat belt, Eric handed the attorney an envelope. "The retainer."

"Just do as you're told," Frank told him as he placed it in his jacket pocket. "Don't argue, don't ask questions or be belligerent in any way. We don't want to inflame the situation."

"My God, Mr. Delmar," Eric said wearily, "I don't even know what the situation really is. Those stupid cops who interviewed me must have known that I had no knowledge of this crime. Like I told you, they didn't even want to look at my DayTimer. They could have taken it with them and done a check to see if the entries matched my whereabouts, but they didn't even bother."

Ten minutes later, they pulled into a parking space in front of a low brick structure with Radcliff Municipal Building, Meriden County, written in Olde English script over the doorway. Its walk was swept clean of snow. Following the signs in the hallway, they approached the front desk where a gaunt-looking sergeant stood eating a jelly donut and watching the replays from the Sunday game on a small portable TV. Ignoring them, he called to a man across the room, "You couldn't get me an extra ticket to the Giants' game, could you, buddy?"

Delmar cleared his throat.

"I'll be right with you," the cop said indulgently, as he reviewed his clipboard. Eric's hands, balled into fists, felt tingly, like they did after hours at the computer.

"Nordblum," the cop finally said, "you gotta go down that hall to be booked, third door on your right."

Eric and Frank followed the directions to the small gray booking room. There were no windows, but the overheads caught them in a trapezoid of fluorescent light.

An older female officer, overflowing her uniform by at least forty pounds, signaled for Eric and Frank to sit at the table opposite her and pushed a pad of paper toward Eric.

While Eric wrote his name, address, height, weight, age, color of hair and eyes, and any distinguishing features in large uneven capital letters, so unlike his usually neat concise script, she sat back in her chair and stared at him accusingly.

"Place of work—why do they have to know where I work?" he asked Frank. If this got out at work, he was finished. Cooked. Destroyed.

"They probably know that already," Frank told him patiently. "Just do what she told you to do."

When he had finished filling out the form, she took a mug shot of him from the front and the side. Eric thought of the time the family was out shopping together at the mall and on the spur of the moment had crammed into a photo booth—how they had made funny faces. That picture was still on the refrigerator.

"Next, your fingerprints," the officer said, as though reading from an instruction manual. Eric listened to her legs rubbing together as she led the way to an even smaller room where Tony Deluca was waiting.

"Hey, I remember you," Eric said belligerently.

Tony smirked as he reached for Eric's hand and started pressing his fingers onto a black ink pad and then onto a form with Eric's name typed across the top. "Boy, your hands are sweaty, aren't they? That tells volumes."

Later, in the men's room, Eric scrubbed and scrubbed at the black ink on his fingers and thought, strangely enough, of his boys, and how Shelly always inspected their hands before sitting down at the table to eat. He wondered if life would ever get back to normal at the Nordblum house.

Before they left, the officer at the front desk called them over and handed Frank some papers. "Your Probable Cause date is February 6th," he told Frank, looking past Eric as though this had nothing to do with him. "You have to fill these out, and get them back to the County Prosecutor, Donna Sheffield. You know the drill," he added in a bored monotone. "Now you gotta go upstairs and post bail. After that, you can leave."

While they waited outside the door of the Central Judicial Processing Courtroom on the second floor, a woman stepped out of the elevator and walked purposely toward Eric and Frank with her hand extended, identifying herself as the county prosecutor. As soon as she said her name, Eric forgot it. They waited then, together, in silence. The bailiff finally signaled them inside and Eric, Frank, and the woman stood before the judge as he read the charges. Assault with a Deadly Weapon and First Degree Larceny.

"Do you understand these charges?"

"Yes, but I never . . ."

"How do you plead?" The judge had already picked up his gavel.

"Not guilty, Your Honor," Eric said. "I have an alibi. Ask anyone, I've never shot a gun in my life . . ." Eric stared straight ahead at the State of New Jersey seal affixed to the front of the judge's bench.

Putting a restraining hand firmly on Eric's arm, Frank immediately requested that Eric be released on his own recognizance while Prosecutor Sheffield voiced-over, pointing out the seriousness of the two charges.

The Judge set bail at ten thousand dollars.

Eric wrote a check from the home equity checkbook that Shelly had given him. Ordinarily, doing something like this, jeopardizing their financial security, would have horrified him, but right now, money had no real meaning to him. Shoving the receipt deep in his pants pocket, he followed Frank back downstairs.

"February 6th?" Eric groaned. "That's months away. I want this horror behind me *now*."

"Be patient," was all Frank could offer.

On the way home, Eric went over everything in his mind, all that had happened in so short a time—Shelly telling him to leave and then giving him another chance, the looks of confusion on the faces of Jason and Arthur. And blurring everything was the memory of those cops, barging into his life, interrogating him, twisting everything he said. Ruining his life.

✺ ✺ ✺

CHAPTER SIXTEEN

Whenever Angelo patted his secretary's tempting rump, his first thought was always of Agnes' saucy little ass before she got sick. The loss of Agnes had enhanced her beauty and intelligence in his mind to the point that no one could ever take her place. On the other hand, Angelo felt sorry for himself. He was a widower, a man alone in the world. Except for Tony. After all he'd suffered, why shouldn't he fondle Shirley? And her sweet rounded bottom fit just right in his plump hand.

"Are you decent, Angelo?" Dan called from the outer office, "I'm coming in . . ."

He laughed as Shirley rushed past him.

"So what does His Honor think about his boy today?" he said, throwing himself in the chair facing Angelo.

"Well, when we assigned him to Gordon's, we certainly never thought he'd be put to the test," Angelo told him. Picking up a couple of paperclips, he stuck them into Tony's silver baby cup. "I don't know how he found Nordblum, and I probably don't want to hear. But I'm not complaining. It'll go a long way, though, in the elections. It's a pretty big thing, for little old Radcliff to break a case of this magnitude."

Angelo was thinking about the cancer drive he had promoted when Agnes was dying. A lot of press had come along with it, but that wasn't why he'd done it. The fact was that he couldn't bear to see her suffer, and for so long. Being a take-action guy, it was the only thing he could think of to do. In the end, it didn't help Agnes, but many other people benefitted, he hoped. He thought back to that early period in their marriage, a time that had been full of love and adventure, campaigning for one office after another with Agnes at his side. Oh, how they had dazzled the crowds. The one brief blemish on that cosmic ride had been completely Angelo's fault and he knew it. Drunk with power and victory, he had strayed. Not a real love affair, but just an infatuation for which he never forgave himself. During that time of confusion and hurt, Agnes had sought solace with someone else. But it had soon been over for both of them and they had sworn never to betray one another again. And they hadn't. Tony was born just nine months later.

Reaching across his desk for a cigar, he clipped it, popped his lighter, and sucked on it until it glowed, while Dan, waving his hand in disgust, went to a window behind his friend's desk and yanked it open. A ribbon of cold air slid into the room.

"I think we'd better get someone from *The Radcliff Record* over to the station for an interview pretty quick," Dan told him.

Angelo knocked the burn off the end of his cigar and laid it carefully in the ashtray. "Well, I think it might be more effective, and give it dignity, if we were to have the press conference right here in my office," he said. "Hell, we could even notify the *New York Daily News,*" he added, warming to the idea.

"Why stop there?" Dan retorted. "How about the Associated Press? Perhaps we could go international with the BBC. Come on, Angelo. For crissake, let's keep this in perspective. The interview will be at the station. You can come if you want to."

"Thanks one whole helluva lot," Angelo told him. "You bet your ass I'll be there, and would you mind closing the damn window?"

"One more thing," Dan said. "I don't know how Tony will handle being interviewed."

"I have no intention of having him talk to the press," Angelo said without hesitation. "I'm the man for that."

* * *

That afternoon, Dan put in a call to Donna Sheffield, even though her office was just one flight up from his own. "How's Radcliff's County Prosecutor doing?" he said.

"Why, just fine, Chief. I bet I know why you're calling. It's about Eric Nordblum. Right?"

"Yup," he told her, picturing her black ringlets that seemed to bounce like loose springs when she turned her head quickly, and that jaunty walk of hers, all hips and ass.

"Wait a sec," she said, "I have his folder right here on my desk. I've been waiting to hear from Frank Delmar, but he hasn't come up with the alibi for his client yet."

"I'd say that means that Nordblum must have a Swiss cheese cover story."

"Yeah, lots of holes in it," they said in unison, both laughing.

Dan could just see her tilting far back in her leather desk chair, maybe propping her sexy black high heels on a pulled-out drawer of her desk. He waited to hear what she had to say next. Whatever it was, it would make sense. She was a smart cookie.

"I guess it's time to cancel the Probable Cause hearing in February and make a date with the Grand Jury," she told Dan. "I'll have the Court put out an arrest warrant."

Knowing Donna, he was sure she was making notes on their conversation. "Where should I send it, Dan?" she asked.

"To Nordblum's Connecticut address," the Chief answered quickly. "That's where Tony told me he's been living since his wife showed him the door."

Dan felt no remorse at not revealing that the tail he had put on Eric had reported that he had moved back to Tolleson. This delay would deprive Eric of whatever advantage he might have had by voluntarily showing up in court with his lawyer the way he did last time. *Then we can arrest the sonofabitch.*

After all, Tony had positive witnesses and Nordblum was about to put the Radcliff police on the map, not just in New Jersey, but in the entire Northeast—wherever there was a Gordon's.

"Shall I proceed with it today?" Donna's voice pulled him back to reality.

"Yup," the Chief agreed, glad she couldn't see the grin on his face. Looking over at Tony who was standing anxiously by the door, he gave him the thumbs-up.

* * *

With the chief's blessing, Tony and Bernie picked up the papers immediately and left for Dalton where they delivered the warrant to the police station which would allow the Connecticut cops to arrest Eric under a Fugitive from Justice Complaint.

By six, they were on their way home, driving west from Dalton with the deepest evening darkness of December pressed against the windows of the cruiser. Small banks of snow lined I-87, but the highway was dry and clear.

"It's great that Nordblum didn't send in that stuff for his alibi," Tony said.

"Why's that?" Bernie asked with a yawn.

"Because, dummy, that's how we've got him under an arrest warrant in Jersey. I knew that calendar thing he waved at us in his apartment was bogus. So what do you think?"

"About what?"

"Come on, Bernie, haven't you been listening? For crying out loud, I'm doing all the thinking here and you can't stay awake long enough to talk to me."

Tony turned off onto Route 4 and was approaching Blandford before Bernie changed the subject. "Hey," he said, sitting up, "let's stop in Huntsville. I know a bar where we can find a couple of broads."

"Sounds like a plan, but right now, I'm hungry," Tony responded.

"Yeah, yeah. I'm saying that we'll stop to eat, and *then* have some fun. What does Mr. Detective think of that?"

Tony spotted four big rigs parked at a restaurant and, knowing that that was usually an indication of good hearty food, he pulled into the snow-swept parking lot fronted by a broken neon sign proclaiming: **I Z Z A.**

"Where's your **P**?" Bernie called to the woman behind the counter as they stomped through the doorway, and then broke out laughing when she pointed at the men's room.

Although Bernie sort of kept things going, Tony was having trouble relaxing. Too much was at stake. He felt as though he was standing on shifting sands, with the tide coming in fast.

✻ ✻ ✻

CHAPTER SEVENTEEN

The minute Frank Delmar came into the office, his legal assistant told him that a Fugitive from Justice Warrant had just come in from the prosecutor on their client, Eric Nordblum.

"That can't be," Frank said. "Sheffield can't do that. We sent all the alibi info to her. Check on the Department of Justice interstate Web site and see if he's listed."

"I didn't get the alibi list from Mr. Nordblum yet, Mr. Delmar," she said, her voice edged with fear. "I . . . I forgot to ask him for it. I'm so sorry. What should I do?" The look on her boss's face cut her off midstream.

"You forgot? You forgot, for crissake? Do you know what that poor man is in for now? You're sorry that Mr. Nordblum will be arrested in three states? And I can't stop it. What the hell did you learn in law school?"

Now she was crying, sobbing out loud.

"Stop that blubbering and get Mr. Nordblum on the phone," he told her. "And don't say one word to him. I'll have to handle this my way and the less he knows about it, the better."

* * *

When Frank called, Eric asked him to wait for a minute. It was, he thought, important for Shelly to listen on another phone. From now on, he didn't trust anyone. So she heard when Frank broke the news that because there were arrest warrants now in New York *and* Connecticut, as well as New Jersey, Eric would have to make an appearance and post bail at all three courthouses.

"Again? My God."

"This is different."

"But we don't have enough cash to do that again." Shelly's voice was shrill.

"You have plenty of time to go to the bank. The courthouse is right on Main Street. I'll drive Eric to Radcliff and you follow with the money."

"Get your sister to go with you," Eric interjected, knowing that if things got out of hand, she could be depended on to quiet Shelly down.

The next morning, Frank once again picked Eric up at his house from which they went directly to the Radcliff police station. On the way, he explained to Eric that, due to a rush to judgment on the part of the prosecutor, there was now a Fugitive from Justice Warrant out for him.

The day was raw and gray, under the threat of low dark clouds. Any time now the sun might break through the lower branches of the trees along the highway or, if it got colder, it might snow. Either way, Eric was dreading what the day would bring.

"Did you receive a Notice of Arrest Warrant?" Frank asked, as they headed toward Radcliff through light traffic.

"Of course not. I didn't get anything. This is all out of the blue."

Frank shook his head. "I smell a skunk and I think its name is Deluca. I'm guessing they delivered the notice to your old address. Deliberately."

"Why would they do something like that? The justice system is supposed to protect, not do sneaky things to ensure an arrest of an innocent man. Deluca didn't care about my DayTimer. He refused to even look at it." Eric's hand was beating a rhythm on the dashboard, emphasizing each thought. He could feel something huge and ugly building inside his chest. "Wait'll the police see it, that should put an end to all this shit."

"There's no explaining what a man will do."

Operating on automatic now, Eric pulled his cell phone out of his pocket and dialed his office. "Something has come up, Maggie," he told her, trying to sound as though everything were normal. "But I'll stop in by the end of today . . ."

He paused because Frank was waving to him to hold a minute.

"We have to go to New York," he told Eric, "and then to Connecticut. You won't be at work until tomorrow."

"On second thought," Eric said without skipping a beat, "I'll see you tomorrow. Thanks, Maggie." And although he had managed to speak as though nothing was wrong, the moment the connection was broken, he sagged forward, like an old man caught in a web of grief.

* * *

"Go upstairs to Courtroom Six," the Radcliff officer announced loudly, looking disparagingly at Eric. "The judge is waiting for you."

Just then, Shelly and her sister, a pale-faced, matronly woman, came rushing through the front doorway. Taking one look at her husband's face, she reached for her sister's hand. At the elevator, Eric kept pushing the up button even though the light was green.

In the courtroom, Judge Herman Barrington read the charges aloud, informing Eric that he was being charged with Assault With a Deadly Weapon and First Class Larceny, having been positively identified as the shooter and one of the three alleged thieves of diamond rings from the Gordon's International department store located in Radcliff, New Jersey on November 29th and further, that there was a Fugitive from Justice Warrant not only in New Jersey but also in New York and Connecticut.

The judge continued talking, but Eric wasn't even listening. As far as he was concerned, the man might just as well have been speaking in another language. But one word got through to him, and that was: *arrested*. He turned and glared at Frank who looked as stunned as Eric felt.

Judge Barrington removed his reading glasses and looked down from the bench. Eric couldn't take his eyes off the judge's hair, wishing for a blast of wind from hell that would unstick those ridiculous strands that were plastered from above one ear all the way to the other.

"For your understanding, Mr. Nordblum, a Fugitive from Justice is one who, having committed a crime within one jurisdiction, goes into another in order to evade the law and avoid its punishment. And I might add that if you identify your partners, things will go easier for you."

"There are no partners," Eric protested. "I live right here in New Jersey. For God's sake, tell him, Frank."

"Your Honor," Frank said, "I represent Mr. Nordblum. The Radcliff police chief told me that there was an arrest warrant out for my client and I assured him that Mr. Nordblum would come in the following morning, voluntarily. And he did. Mr. Nordblum is *not* a Fugitive from Justice, Your Honor."

"It is the finding of this bail hearing," the judge stated, ignoring Frank, "that based on this affidavit from the Radcliff Police Department, I am setting bail at ten thousand dollars for the Assault with a Deadly Weapon and the First Class Larceny Warrants and a bond for forty thousand dollars for the Fugitive from Justice Warrant. Until your client makes bail, he must remain in custody. Now, Counselor, what do you have to say?" he added, looking up.

"My client is not a flight risk, Your Honor," Attorney Delmar said firmly. "He is a family man and a most respected member of his community. He did not commit these crimes. He has an ironclad alibi. Furthermore, Mr. Nordblum never received the warrant. It must have been served at his temporary address in Connecticut."

"If your client is innocent, the truth will come out," the judge continued dismissively, "but for now, bail must be paid. Is there anything further to come before the court?"

"No, Your Honor."

"The only diamond ring I ever had in my hand is when I married my wife fifteen years ago," Eric protested, aiming his comment at the floor.

A court officer stepped forward and started to take Eric by his arm. Ambushed by an intense rush of rage, Eric jerked his arm out of his grasp.

"Eric! Mr. Delmar!" Shelly called out from the seat behind them, frantically waving a checkbook in the air. "I have the money. I can pay the bail, Judge. Who do I give the money to? Here it is!" Eric thought she cried out with a passion that made her almost sound unhinged.

In the end, the bailiff told Shelly to follow him and that he would explain everything. Eric thought he heard Shelly say that there was no way she wanted to pledge their home as collateral. Pledge their home? For God's sake, it's still mortgaged. *How had he gotten into the middle of this mess?*

Ultimately, Eric had to wait in a jail cell for over an hour before the bail payment was settled. In spite of aching legs, he stood up the entire time, not wanting to touch anything, not wanting to acknowledge that he was even there, in this filthy, stinking place. Blocking out the sound of someone moaning in the next cell, he had a vision of his bed. His and Shelly's. How secure he felt there. How he wanted to *be* there. This whole thing was impossible. A great empty mistake. He was caught up in a vortex of lies and couldn't imagine how to escape it.

But the truth, Eric now knew without question, revealed that he was the defendant in a criminal proceeding in not one, but in three states.

* * *

Eric, completely drained, sank back against the seat as Frank sped the Mercedes toward the interstate, out into farm country, past silver-topped silos gleaming like spaceships, dairy farms, 200-year-old houses, and hayfields white with crusted snow and closed his eyes to discourage conversation.

Since Frank was not a member of the New York bar, he had made arrangements for an attorney from that state to meet them at the Kensington Police Department. However, before they could proceed, Eric had to write him a check for $2,000 as a retainer. The two lawyers sat in the back of the room talking quietly, like they were at a goddamn tea party, while Eric went through the same humiliating procedure of being booked as a felon and treated like a mindless criminal. Do this, do that. What would the boys think of him if they saw him here? He had always tried to do the right thing, live a clean life, set a proper example. But, due to no fault of his own, he had been rendered impotent by a system he now hated.

This time, he was locked in a jail cell for almost three unbearable hours waiting for Shelly to show up with the bail money. She brought cash *and* the checkbook, clearly so confused and upset that she was not at all sure what was required. He sat on the edge of the wooden chair in the cell, rigid and silent, his hands capping his knees as he watched the tide of shadows that rose from the floor, every few seconds glancing at his watch. In the end, Eric departed the courthouse not having spoken more than ten words to his New York attorney.

On the way to Connecticut, they drove in tandem, Frank and Eric leading the way with Shelly and Robin following. Having missed lunch, they had agreed to stop for a bite along the turnpike. Unable to think about anything, let alone food, Eric waited in his attorney's car, seething.

After another retainer had been paid to a Connecticut attorney, the entire booking procedure was repeated in Dalton, only this time the bail was paid more quickly and they were all on their way to their respective homes by seven that same night. It had been the longest day that Eric had ever known.

Heading back to Tolleson, Shelly drove, with Robin sitting in the front next to her. She told Eric, who was slumped in the back with his eyes closed, about her frantic dash to the bank for additional bail money—how she had first taken it out of the wrong account and how frightened she was. Eric wasn't listening.

* * *

CHAPTER EIGHTEEN

On Wednesday, the Nordblum household followed their regular early morning routines as though the previous day had never happened. At six o'clock, the coffee was brewing and Eric was shaved, showered, and dressed for work. As usual, the boys had to be called three times before coming down for breakfast. Since Shelly didn't have to be at the library until ten, she was still in her bathrobe as she fixed his breakfast, having already made lunches for herself and the boys and packed them in brown bags. Conversation centered on homework and basketball. By six-thirty, Eric was out the door and on the road to Dalton.

Checking in his rearview mirror, he saw the same dark green car directly behind him, not even attempting to follow at a discreet distance. What the hell did they think they were going to see? Usually Eric didn't mind the traffic, but today, in spite of it, he pushed eighty and tailgated every car in his way. He was rushing to work, to act—*normal*—*as if his life was not falling apart.* He entered the Dalton Industrial Park a bit too fast and had to jam his brakes when, *who was it? Oh God, it was Maggie that had stopped in front of him.* Eric honked and waved with a half-smile.

Going straight to his office, he closed the door and dialed Frank Delmar's private number. "What happens next?" he asked the minute Frank came on the line.

"Who is this?"

"The guy you spent all day with yesterday, the guy who could go to jail for something he didn't do. I need to know what the next step is. I have an alibi, for crissake."

"Of course I know who you are, Eric. I was going to call you this morning." There was a rustling of papers before Frank continued. "I just got word by fax confirming that the prosecutor will be handling the presentation of your case at the Radcliff County Court and reminding us that the February court date has been cancelled."

"What has it been changed to?" Eric shouted. Jesus, it's like the movies, he thought, only Hollywood wasn't going to fix the ending for him. Nobody was.

"As soon as a new date is scheduled, she'll let us know. Please try to take things in stride, Eric. I'll call her back this morning to tell her that your alibi will cover all of the pertinent times of the alleged crimes."

"I thought you had already handled that."

"Yes. Well, we're taking care of it now." Frank's tone seemed to change, but Eric couldn't quite get why. Was Delmar hiding some loophole in the screwed-up legal system that would deem his alibi inadmissible? "All we need is that DayTimer of yours. And, of course, your telephone bills. Can you get those into the mail today?"

"And will that settle it once and for all? That's it? That's all I have to do? Because, if that's all you need, why didn't you ask for it before?" And then, when Frank didn't reply, "Okay, that will go out today."

For the first time since this horrible travesty had begun, Eric could only imagine his DayTimer might finally put an end to it. Looking through the worn pages made him feel grateful that he had always been so meticulous, recording in detail all his business meetings and activities every day. *Could he dare to hope it would soon be over?*

* * *

Grabbing his telephone bills and his DayTimer, and telling Maggie that he would be back in twenty minutes, Eric drove downtown to the Dalton post office, addressed an envelope to Attorney Frank Delmar in Trenton, and stood in line to post it.

On his way out of the parking lot, Eric came to a sudden stop when he realized that he had just mailed his only copy—the only proof of his alibi. Re-parking the car, he ran back into the post office, rushed past a line of people, and told the clerk who had waited on him that he needed to have the package he had just mailed, only to be told to get back in line and wait his turn.

Eric glared at the back of every person ahead of him until he was at the counter. "I'm the one who wants to get a package back that I just mailed. It was bubble-wrapped inside a priority envelope."

"I can't do that, sir," the man answered.

Eric wanted to reach across the counter and strangle him.

By the time he got back to the office, *without* his DayTimer, everyone had left for lunch. What kind of a fool was he not to have made a copy, Eric asked himself. He always made copies of everything, in business and at home.

If that package went missing, who would believe him? And if no one believed him, he could be put in jail without bail, stuck there indefinitely.

* * *

CHAPTER NINETEEN

Shelly watched Eric pull into the driveway just in time for dinner. It certainly wasn't lost on her that he had adjusted his travel schedule so that he could eat with the family almost every night. Since his days started earlier, his workday must have become grueling. It was okay with her for him to suffer a little. She didn't want him to think he could ever cheat on her again and get away with it. This was the end of the line as far as she was concerned. Frankly, she hoped she hadn't made his return too easy.

An arrest warrant was serious. She knew that. They didn't do something like that without being pretty damn certain. But it was insanity to think that Eric could be involved. *Wasn't it?*

Once his terrible near-disaster appeared to be under control, Eric continued to try to repair their lives. Starting with the first week, he jammed with his jazz group on Tuesday, and he'd even attended church with the family which was something he usually left up to her to do. It was clear that he wouldn't be satisfied with just restoring the status quo. He wanted their marriage to be stronger than it had ever been.

But it was incredible how sneaky little thoughts could creep under your skin and into your subconscious to undermine what you were doing. That's why Shelly insisted on marriage counseling, and, to her surprise, Eric didn't resist.

Getting ready for bed that evening, Shelly couldn't stop herself. "Are you absolutely positive, Eric, that this theft has nothing to do with you?"

"My God. What are you saying? That you think I robbed and shot someone?"

"No, but it's such a mystery that they picked you out of all the hundreds of criminals that could have done it."

"I thought you were behind me in this fight."

"I am. Of course I am. It's just such a weird thing."

When they made love now, instead of comforting her, it was, well, alarming. Because it seemed that he was trying too hard, being too gentle, too considerate . . . *or maybe his mind was somewhere else.*

She was okay with him feeling humbled and grateful. Forgiving is one thing; forgetting is another.

Even in the half-light, Shelly saw the tiny smudges of shadows beneath his eyes and then she gave herself over to the quiet repair of sleep. Outside, the sky wept.

* * *

Eric picked up the mail and carried it into the kitchen where Shelly was preparing dinner. Since he had returned home, everything had been positive, until just now when he received a registered letter from Frank Delmar stating that, as a civil trial lawyer, he could no longer represent Eric since his had turned into a felony case. He added some encouraging comments and enclosed a list of criminal defense lawyers, telling Eric that he would forward all information to his new representative as soon as Eric let him know which one he had chosen. "Good luck," was his closing comment.

It came over Eric so quickly. The feeling that he was going to explode, as if his anger had grown so big and so fast that it would choke him. He wanted to put his fist into Frank's face. Drive to his office and do it. He threw the letter in Shelly's direction and she let it drift to the floor.

"Now we have to start all over," Eric told her, his voice rising, out of control. He followed her into the dining room as she calmly continued to prepare for the meal. "Let's see, we've only paid *two* bloodsucking lawyers plus Delmar so far," he told her, even though she didn't appear to be listening. "Now we need another one to coordinate my defense. It should be easy. After all, I'm only being charged in three states. My defense shouldn't cost much. And who cares, anyway? The boys can work their way through college." He thought he could smell something burning in the kitchen, but neither one of them moved to investigate.

He could tell from the alarmed look in Shelly's eyes that she was really startled. And no wonder. He had always been so calm and even-tempered, never indulging in violent outbursts. He was relieved when she hurried into the kitchen.

Eric looked at his wife's retreating back and soon he could hear the jangle of silverware and the clank of plates as she set the table. Only then did he bend down and pick up the letter.

* * *

The next day he began the search. One New York lawyer he interviewed told Eric that he had defended twelve murderers. When Eric started to assure him that he was certainly not involved with the Gordon's shooting nor with any robberies, he retorted, "Listen, I don't care whether you did it or not. I'm here to get you off."

Eric couldn't relate to that kind of thinking. That night, he told Shelly that he hated all attorneys. "All they think about is their fee."

"I don't care what it costs at this point," Shelly told him impatiently. "Get the *best* lawyer. I want this behind us." There was, he thought, something different in her voice.

This time when Eric referred to Frank's list, another name popped out at him. It was someone that he had seen on television; David Rothberg, a big-time, high profile, New York criminal lawyer who was famous for winning his cases no matter whom he was defending. If Shelly wanted to go for broke, the hell with it; that was who he'd choose.

Suddenly, Eric remembered that Delmar had his DayTimer. *He had to get it back from him, if the bastard hadn't already lost it. Would this nightmare ever end?*

Another sleepless night. Why? Because he had had a sudden and horrifying memory of buying Shelly a string of cultured pearls for her thirtieth birthday and it might have been at a Gordon's. *Holy shit, it was at Gordon's.* If they ever found out that he had lied about not shopping there, then they wouldn't believe anything he had said.

I didn't lie deliberately, I just forgot.

* * *

On December twenty-second, another Gordon's was hit. "Maybe the other two perps decided to grab some loot on their own," Tony said to Bernie across their desk when he read about it on the teletype. The words were no sooner out of his mouth when a call came in from a Detective Callahan of the Tolleson Police Department asking about the case.

Without hesitation, Tony immediately told him how he had single-handedly nailed the shooter, the scam leader, a man named Eric Nordblum. Tony also let him know that there was a warrant out for Eric's arrest.

"Yeah, I saw it," Detective Callahan said. "The guy lives right here in Tolleson, you know."

"He does?" Tony said, making his tone sound innocent. "Well, *we* found him when he was living in Connecticut, the same town where he works, and now, where this latest robbery occurred. I was just reading about it." He stood up and turned away from Bernie, stretching the cord as far as it would extend.

"Yeah, pretty dumb of the guy, I mean, making a hit in Dalton. But since he's moved back to Tolleson, why don't we pick him up for you this afternoon under the new warrant and then we'll hand him over to you guys tomorrow morning," Callahan suggested, excitedly. "What do you think?"

"I'll check with my chief and get right back to you," Tony told him, suddenly not sure how enthusiastic he actually felt with this development. This ratcheted up the ante, he thought; moved it out of his control. *What had he set in motion? Nordblum wouldn't do something that incriminating, would he?*

Walking slowly down the hallway to Dan's office, Tony pushed open the door and announced that the Tolleson Department wanted to pick up Nordblum.

"When?"

"Right now."

"It's just before Christmas," Dan reminded him. "It could sway sympathy toward him." If the truth were known, Tony bet that the chief couldn't care less about Christmas or Eric Nordblum, but he *did* care about public opinion.

"That's what's good about letting *them* pick him up," Tony told him. "It'll be the Tolleson cops, not us. Once they've got Nordblum, they'll keep him overnight and then transfer him over here." He leaned toward Dan expectantly, holding up his hands as if absolving himself of any responsibility, any wrongdoing. Let Dan make this decision, he thought nervously.

"That could work. Yeah, it's an idea," Dan conceded. "Do you want me to let Tolleson know we're on board?"

"No, I'll take care of it, Chief. Hey, are you keeping His Honor current on my detective work?"

"Get out of here," Dan told him impatiently. "Is that all you think of, impressing your father? Don't you know that nothing ever gets past him?"

Tony returned to his desk knowing there was no going back now. He grabbed the phone and dialed Callahan, telling him to go ahead and pick up Nordblum. "Call me when you've got him."

"We won't bring him over to you till late tomorrow morning. Maybe if he's scared enough, he'll turn in his accomplices," Callahan said.

Tony needed to set aside his fears. This was the kind of success he had dreamed of and he just knew that Pop, and Dan, too, couldn't be anything but impressed in a big way. This called for a drink. With as much bravado as he could muster, he squared his shoulders and switched on the intercom.

"Hey Detective Pigeon. Are you available for a cold one over at Billy's?"

"Shut off that thing," Bernie said, coming out of the head.

"We did it, Bernie! We bagged him. Nordblum's headed for the Tolleson tank as we speak. They're delivering him to us in the morning. Tonight, we celebrate!" He picked up an open can of Coke, guzzled it straight down, and belched loudly, looking over at Bernie to see if he'd gotten a laugh out of him.

* * *

Two days before Christmas, Eric had gone home from Dalton early to help Jason and Arthur wrap some secret Christmas gifts for Shelly. Bing Crosby was delivering "White Christmas" from a CD, while Eric was pouring eggnog in the kitchen. No booze in his, not until Shelly came home. It had been fun shopping with the boys, watching them choose something that would please their mother. They were fooling around now by draping silver icicles over their heads, crooning along with Bing.

Eric was just passing the scotch tape to Jason when someone started hammering on the front door. "Santa is early," he laughed over his shoulder. As Eric pulled open the door, two big Tolleson police officers, led by Detective Callahan, pushed their way inside. "Are you Eric Nordblum?" he demanded.

When Eric nodded, they flung him against the wall.

"What the hell?" Eric said in a voice he didn't recognize. It was trembly and falsetto. While his sons hugged one another and cried, the cops frisked him, handcuffed him, and read him his rights. Eric heard *deadly weapon* and *fugitive*—words flying around like hornets, and then they hauled him away in a police cruiser, lights flashing and siren blaring, drawing his neighbors to their windows. "Call your mother at the library," Eric yelled.

✢ ✢ ✢

CHAPTER TWENTY

Once again, Shelly was galvanized into action. Dashing home to grab the checkbook, she rushed to get to the bank before it closed at five. After withdrawing $3,000, she drove straight downtown to the police department. At first, they wouldn't let her see her husband, but reluctantly, they finally relented, giving her a few minutes.

"Why? Why?" she cried to Eric. He could tell that she was trying not to breathe in the stench of the cell.

"How should I know? This is hideous. They're taking me to the Radcliff police station in the morning. Go home, Shel. Tell the kids I'm okay. Go home and wait till I call you."

"What about this money?"

"I don't know anything," he told her. "I guess they don't want it yet. The only thing I *do* know is that I have to stay in a stinking rat hole overnight. They've taken my cell phone, even my belt for crissake. Go to the boys. Call Maggie. Tell her I'm sick and won't be available tomorrow. Very sick. I don't want anyone to know about this."

* * *

"Name?" barked the bored-looking recording officer at the reception desk.

"Nordblum," Eric said in a rusty voice, his heart thumping.

"Height, weight, eyes . . . .?" Eric watched his answers being scrawled across the booking card. Next, a guard led him to a room the size of a walk-in closet; empty, except for a desk and a row of shelves stacked with prison-issue clothing. "Strip," the officer said.

"Come on," Eric pleaded, "I have an alibi. My wife will bring the bail. You don't need to do this." Knowing he was about to be strip-searched and locked up when he had been wrongfully accused was making him tremble with hatred.

"Yeah, yeah, everyone says that they're innocent. No one wants to strip. No one wants to be deloused," the cop told him. "But everyone's gotta. It's standard procedure. Now drop your shorts and bend over." Struggling out of his chair, he pulled on his rubber gloves, snapping them onto his hands menacingly.

After he had surrendered to that humiliation, Eric was ushered through the barred gate separating them from the holding cells. His footsteps echoed down the long concrete corridor as the derelicts behind bars were calling out insults. The tiny solitary cell, five-by-nine feet, was filled with a powerful stink coming from a lidless corroded urinal in the corner. The cell reeked of booze and vomit and human waste, the legacy of the last inmate who had been confined there.

After the iron door clanged shut behind him, Eric, whose orange coveralls smelled strongly of bleach, held his breath and tried not to be sick. He thought he had learned what jail was like last time, but this was different, a greater debasement, given without conscience or meaning. He sank down on the edge of the filthy metal bunk; the odor of despair settled around him.

They had even taken his glasses away from him.

He looked up at the narrow window near the ceiling, hazy with grime, and thought he saw the first few snowflakes of a predicted blizzard. When he was a child, everyone said that the person who saw the first flake would have their wish granted. Closing his eyes, he made a wish, but he doubted if anyone was listening.

* * *

Early the next morning, when the local newspaper was delivered to Eric's cell along with a breakfast of stale shredded wheat and lukewarm coffee, he discovered that his arrest was all over the front page: *TOLLESON MAN ARRESTED, ALLEGED GUNMAN/THIEF AT GORDON'S INTERNATIONAL DEPARTMENT STORE. Eric Nordblum of 314 North Main Street in Tolleson was arrested in his home.*

So everyone would know now. Strangely enough, Eric found that it did not bother him as much as the memory of his children sobbing as he had been led away, a memory that he knew would haunt him all his life long.

* * *

When they pulled into the Radcliff Police parking lot at about ten the next morning, Eric saw Tony waiting by the side door.

"Come on out of there, Nordblum," Callahan growled, "they've been waiting for you."

It was difficult for Eric to get out of the back seat due to being handcuffed, and when he did, the eight inches of new snow covering the walk immediately seeped into his unlaced dress shoes. I am not here, he thought dizzily as he shuffled beside Callahan. I'm lying on my back, sleeping on a beach somewhere in the sun with Shelly and the boys, and this is just a horrible dream. Lurching across the unbroken snow, he stumbled and went down on one knee.

Two uniformed officers who were standing on either side of the door, their hands resting lightly on their holstered sidearms, laughed as though they were watching comedy hour.

"Cut the shit," Callahan said to him, pulling Eric roughly to his feet. He threw Tony a plastic bag in which Eric's clothes and personal belongings were stuffed.

"He's been whining about his glasses," he said. "They're in there somewhere. You can send the jumpsuit back any time. Laundered, of course," he added, laughing shrilly.

"Thanks, buddy, I won't forget this," Tony replied, and then, feeling magnanimous, "hey, a bunch of us're going deer hunting tomorrow early, want to come?"

"Nah, I already got mine," Callahan said, getting back in his cruiser, "thanks anyway."

Eric waited, shivering from the cold. He was afraid because there was no way he could protect himself. Looking at Tony, he knew that he had never truly hated anyone until now. It was a feeling as pure as love. And yet, not even twenty minutes later, his face expressionless, Tony handed him his glasses through the cell bars.

＊ ＊ ＊

Shelly had been waiting all night for another call from Eric. The one phone call he would be allowed was, of course, to her. She needed to find out what to do about posting bail.

"Come *now*, Shelly. Bring cash."

"Where are you?"

"I'm in Radcliff. Oh Christ, get me out of here."

Although it was only twenty miles from Tolleson to Radcliff, because of the snow and a short detour to pick up Robin, Shelly thought she'd never get there. When they entered the Radcliff station forty-five minutes later, she announced why she was there to a cocky-looking cop who must be Deluca, who was sitting at a table enjoying coffee and donuts. Taking the envelope containing the bail money from her, he tossed it to another cop he called Bernie and told him to count it. There were three other police officers standing around, watching. One said; "Wow, this guy Nordblum must really be involved in something big for you to have this kind of money hanging around." He winked at Robin, and added, "Probably drugs."

Shelly pretended to ignore the comment, although she could feel the vertical crease between her eyes, one that had not been there a month ago, deepen. How had Eric gotten her into such a demeaning situation? She vowed silently never to pay in cash again no matter what was happening to him. *God forbid that there should ever be another time.*

"Yeah, it's all here," Bernie finally said, handing the money back to her after counting it twice. "Take it to that desk over there and they'll send the message down to release your husband."

Nothing had turned out the way she had hoped it would once she'd allowed Eric to come back home. At first, things had gone pretty well, with him trying so hard to be what she wanted. But even then, it hadn't been the same. Maybe he had been trying too hard, or maybe she wanted something different from him. Then there was always the question of *trust*. And now, this. Could the cops have something on Eric that in her wildest dreams she would not have been able to predict? Or believe?

Shelly really didn't know if she could take any more of this. Everything had changed between her and Eric and she couldn't imagine what path they could take to return them to where they had been a year ago.

☆ ☆ ☆

CHAPTER TWENTY-ONE

Eric and Shelly's appointment had been delayed by nearly two weeks due to the holidays, but finally they were sitting at a massive walnut desk across from Attorney David Rothberg. His posh office on the fifth floor of the Zeckendorf Towers in New York City was furnished with period antiques, mostly dark walnut, very ornate, with floor-to-ceiling windows overlooking Union Square. Everything was paid for by suckers like him, Eric thought, taking note of the desk chair which featured intricately carved lion heads with claws curling over the hand rests.

Rothberg, a handsome man in his early fifties, exuded confidence. There was a smell that Eric couldn't quite identify. Cigar? Imported furniture polish? His own fear?

"Let's get the rough stuff out of the way first," the lawyer said pleasantly. "My retainer is $15,000 to be paid today. Then I can dig in."

Eric hoped Rothberg didn't notice the way his hand was shaking when he calmly wrote out a check on their home equity account. Years ago, Shelly had insisted that they establish it, for emergencies only, she had argued, and now it was nearly at the limit. Eric knew he was approaching *his* limit. How could he keep up his campaign to win Shelly's trust back and at the same time shake this anonymous threat off his back?

"Okay," Rothberg said, as he opened his desk drawer and dropped the check inside. "From what I understand from Attorney Delmar, this may be a grievous account of perjury on the part of the officers who signed and swore to the affidavit that caused your wrongful arrest. If this is so, it becomes a clear case of reckless indifference to your right to be considered innocent unless proven guilty."

Maybe, Eric thought, he's the one who will make this all go away. My life depends on him. Maybe it's not too late.

"Since I am a member of the New Jersey bar," Rothberg told him, "I'll be working as lead attorney and will coordinate your defense with your other counsel."

"You know that Frank Delmar dropped our case," Eric said woodenly, his hopes plummeting.

"Of course, that's why you're here," Rothberg said, without missing a beat. "Now, what I need from you, Mr. Nordblum, is that DayTimer you told me about, as well as your phone records for the time line surrounding the shooting and the robbery."

"I don't have my DayTimer," Eric muttered, his voice barely perceptible now. "I sent it to Delmar."

"I'm surprised you didn't make a copy of it. But don't worry; we'll get it from him. I also need to know of anyone who could attest to your whereabouts specifically on the day of the robbery. Will that be a problem?"

Eric stared at Rothberg's dark curly hair and found his mind wandering. It was difficult to even begin to contemplate the consequences of allowing his new lawyer to contact his customers and fellow workers.

"Mr. Nordblum?"

Eric started. "Yes, yes, I can give that to you but," he asked distractedly, "could your inquiries be circumspect? I mean, these are people I work with—doing business with them is what pays my salary."

Eric rose abruptly, still with his winter coat on, and started to pace in front of the desk, ignoring Shelly's expression that was clearly signaling him to sit down. He knew what he must look like, face flushed, his dark hair wet with perspiration.

"Why can't *you* just look at my DayTimer and see for yourself where I was and what I was doing on that damn day?" he protested. "Those cops just picked me out at random and hung this thing on me with no evidence. I HAVE AN ALIBI. Alibi means *elsewhere*, doesn't it? It proves I wasn't there." Eric removed his glasses and rubbed his eyes that had gone out of focus with rage.

Shelly pulled at his arm, "Please, Eric," was all she said. Dropping into his chair, he slumped down until he was resting on his spine. The nugget of hard black pity in his wife's eyes hurt as much as anything she might have said to him.

"The truth doesn't care what we think of it, Mr. Nordblum," Rothberg said in a lecture-like tone. "Proof is what counts with the law and alibi has a specific, honorable meaning: I could not have performed this crime because I was somewhere else."

"Honorable? Ha! There's nothing honorable about this farce."

Ignoring the comment, the lawyer continued, "Therefore, you're right, Mr. Nordblum. Alibi does indeed mean elsewhere."

Picking up Eric's folder, he straightened it by tapping the edge and then set it down precisely aligned with the upper right hand corner of his desk before rising with his hand extended.

"So, you'll get that information to me ASAP?" he asked in a tone that clearly ended their meeting. "Remember, the wheels of justice tend to turn slowly."

✣ ✣ ✣

CHAPTER TWENTY-TWO

On days that he didn't make sales calls, Eric had been arriving at the main office in Dalton earlier and earlier. Today, it was five-fifteen. He hardly remembered the commute, traveling the nearly traffic-free highway through the bleak February landscape. There had been one snow squall, a kind of fine dancing dust that rose up without weight across his windshield and disappeared. The ever-present green car stayed at a not-even-cautious distance behind. Eric wondered how much the driver was getting paid for his vigil.

Sleep was a mirage, a wavy line always in the distance and it showed around Eric's eyes. Delmar had sent the DayTimer and phone records directly to Rothberg's office which had been a good start, but now, three weeks had passed and still nothing. Eric was coming to the painful discovery that living in limbo was devastating. He couldn't concentrate on anything. His only refuge was his office where he could breathe the anesthetic of work.

Maggie always came in at quarter to nine to get the coffeepot going, open the mail, and be at her desk at nine sharp. She worked with the other salesmen, although, being the top performer for the past three years, Eric got most of her attention.

This morning, when she arrived at the office, she tossed her golden-brown hair back from her face and stared at him for an uncomfortable moment. Whenever she had something important to say, it seemed that the sprinkle of freckles across her nose became more prominent.

"What?"

"There's been talk."

"About?"

"A detective from over in Jersey was nosing around yesterday, asking a lot of personal questions about you."

"Step into my office, will you?" Even though there was no one close enough to hear, he shut the door. "What's his name?"

Maggie checked a notepad in her hand. "Tony Deluca."

"Jesus. *Him*. What kind of questions?"

"Like, have you given me a diamond ring? And did I know if you own a gun."

"My God, that man is unbelievable."

"He also asked if you'd ever had a mustache and if I had seen you wear gold cuff links studded with diamonds. Gee, Eric, I'm really sorry to tell you this, but I thought you'd want to know. Never mind him. He's a slime-ball. I told him to leave and not to come back."

"Did he?"

"Yes, he did. But unfortunately, I saw him headed toward Mr. Johansen's office."

Eric felt the blood drain from his face. Hastily gathering up the papers on his desk, he shoved them into his briefcase.

"I have a couple of calls to make and then I'll be working in my home office," he told her. "If anyone wants me, take a message. Please, Maggie, I can't talk to anyone right now."

"I understand. And I just want you to know that I believe in you. I always will." Eric could see that she wanted to know more and he also knew she would sympathize with whatever he told her. But he couldn't risk exposing his pain to anyone who showed concern, especially Maggie; it might result in his breaking down, and above all, he needed to contain his anger and stay strong.

Just as he headed out the door, Mr. Johansen, the CEO, stopped Eric in the hall, barring his escape. "I'd like to see you in my office," he said, striding on ahead, not even looking to see if he was following.

Once seated behind his desk, he waved Eric into the chair opposite him.

"I'm going to get right to the point," he said, his face expressionless. "You know that you must have a squeaky clean background in order to have government clearance in this job. Squeaky clean. Pristine," he emphasized. "This thing that's going on with you has destroyed your legitimacy with us here at MTS. Whether the allegations are true or not doesn't matter. Once the accusation is made, you're finished with this company. And any other job that requires clearance."

The bastard didn't even have the courage to look him straight in the eye. A creeping nausea rose in Eric's throat as his words sunk in. "But I didn't do anything, Mr. Johansen. I have alibis for all of this. I was working, for God's sake."

"Unfortunately, that doesn't matter," Johansen replied, starting to fidget with the papers on his desk.

"What do you mean it doesn't matter? Haven't I been your top salesman for the last three years? Doesn't that count for anything?"

"Yes, you have, and of course that matters," he said, a barely detectable edge creeping into his voice. "We're grateful to you for your past performance, but this company cannot sustain adverse publicity. Put yourself in my place, Eric. You'd do the same thing."

"The hell I would. What did Deluca say? Did he tell you that he and his lackey made up the whole story probably to cover up bad police work? My God, one day you're slapping me on the back and the next day you're kicking me out."

"Come on now, Eric," Johansen said nervously, reaching for the telephone. "You just calm down. Go back to your office and gather any personal items, right now. We discussed your crime, uh, alleged crime that is, at the board meeting and we're willing to offer you a four-week severance package, with six months of health insurance coverage. That's generous, all things considered."

Eric wanted to kick Johansen, violently, a desire so fierce that it was all he could do to control himself. He pictured Johansen lying on the floor begging for mercy.

Fifteen minutes later, Eric, with a small box of personal items under his arm, was being escorted out of the building by security. Once in his car, shivering in the cold of late winter, he locked the doors and slept for three hours in the parking lot.

For the next couple of weeks, this is what he did. Left home for work on time, drove around, and slept in his car.

* * *

"Don't lie to me, Eric Nordblum," Shelly said slowly, her voice hard as a spike. "If Mr. Johansen has talked to you about what's happening, I need to know. For God's sake, Eric, you may lose your job."

She thought of their early years, especially after the boys were born, when their lives had been smooth and predictable. Suddenly, she could feel everything in the house changing, a coldness passing through the white linen walls, invading the rooms, fluttering pages of the boys' school books, passing over the dishes in the sink.

Anxiety had shrunken Eric's face and caved in his mouth. When he tried to put his arms around her, she jerked away from him and began pacing furiously about the room, touching things at random, unable to force herself to look directly at him.

"We were doing pretty well, and now this," she said. "We've quit counseling. You haven't gone to church in weeks. You haven't touched your clarinet—we don't *talk* to each other anymore. You're gone from the house before the boys and I even wake up." She knew that she must sound as though she was reading from a list, but she couldn't help herself.

"I'm sorry," he said. The effort of speaking those two words seemed to alter something in him. He sat down in a chair and let his head fall back, his hands slack along the upholstery.

"I can't take it any longer." She was shocked to hear such venom in her own voice. Her fingers were shredding a plastic bag which she held in her hand for some unknown reason. She stretched it and made holes.

"Okay, you want the truth?" Eric demanded with such forcefulness that she was startled. "Well, here it is," he told her. "I've been fired. Is that what you wanted to hear?"

She dropped down onto a footstool feeling as though she had been punched in the stomach. "That's what I suspected," she said. Every fiber of her being focused on the task of not screaming. She could feel the pressure behind her eyelids, at the base of her nose, in her jaw. She began slowly, making sure her voice didn't shake or throb in any way.

"Well, I'm sorry for you, Eric," she told him. "I'm sorry for both of us. I assume you didn't rob those stores, but I just can't help thinking that, in some crazy way, all this is your own fault."

Her words fell between them like a rain of arrows.

"I can't live this way. Our marriage is doomed. We are *this* far from a divorce," Shelly pinched her index finger and her thumb close to her face. She looked past her husband, into the kitchen where the faucet was leaking. *I'll have to fix it myself.*

Suddenly Eric began to cry. He sat at the edge of the couch and curled inward, his face in his lean hard hands, his head falling downward into the pale blue of his shirt. Shelly stood, and, feeling dizzy, walked with small steps toward the window, straightening a pillow on the couch in passing.

"You don't mean that, Shel," Eric pleaded finally. "We need to be close, to be partners, to make love. Please Shelly, if you ever cared, please show me you love me."

As the seconds passed, she looked at him as though she didn't understand what he was saying, but then, in silent agreement, Shelly followed Eric into their bedroom. That last attempt to make love vandalized whatever shred of romance might have been left in their marriage.

* * *

CHAPTER TWENTY-THREE

"How do I look?" Tony asked Bernie as he stood by their desk wearing a new leather jacket flapping open over his chest, designer jeans, and powder-blue dress shirt starched stiff like the ones he wore with his uniform.

"Like a pro," Bernie told him. "When did the chief say we could kick the uniforms?"

Tony picked up a memo addressed to him on his desk. "What's this? Nordblum's Pontiac is going to be impounded? Who ordered that?"

"Chief."

"When?"

"This morning."

Shit. I was planning to do that yesterday.

Someone snickered in the next cubicle.

"Laugh all you want, assholes," Tony shouted good-naturedly, glossing over the memo, "but I'm the one getting the promotion."

"When did this happen? And what about me, Tony?" Bernie sat down and leaned across their desk. His hostility was sudden and unmistakable. "You promised that if I went along with that affidavit you concocted, you'd see to it that I'd get promoted, too."

Tony lowered his voice. "Of course I recommended you. But I'm warning you right now, don't you *ever* talk about that affidavit again. The one, I might remind you, we *both* signed."

"I can't believe I ever signed that friggin' thing—stuck my neck way out for you."

"Hold your horses, Bernie. I spoke to the Chief *and* His Honor on your behalf. Detective's in the bag for both of us, so stop worrying. Besides, you're just jealous of my new duds."

Tony laughed in a nervous loud bark to let him know it was a joke, of course, but Bernie didn't smile. Even when Tony reached out and gave him a tentative pat on the shoulder, he had a feeling that things would never be quite the same between them again.

* * *

Dan hurried down Main Street to O'Malley's where, as was their Friday custom, he was meeting Angelo for lunch. He preferred Sherman's Diner, but Angelo liked to spread their patronage around town and besides, this was where the Republicans who supported him hung out.

The waitress, who had worked at O'Malley's since forever, slapped two laminated menus of lunch specials down in front of them.

"Hello, gentlemen," she said, standing with one hand on her hip. "You having your regulars?"

They both nodded.

"I hear the Bureau is involved in the string of Gordon's robberies now that they are multi-state crimes," Angelo said as she headed for the kitchen. "A case of this magnitude, especially since Radcliff was the only location where there was a shooting, could carry us further than we had ever expected. Governor Deluca. *Senator Deluca . . .*" The titles rolled off his tongue.

Shaking his head, Dan grinned at the massive ego sitting across from him. "And what did you have in mind for me? I'm supposed to ride your coattail, to what? Security Chief . . .?"

"Oh hell, I'm just dreaming," Angelo said. "What did you tell the boys about missing the latest news conference?"

"That I didn't know you had set it up for the day they'd be out of town."

"Thanks a lot, my friend. That's one more thing Tony'll be pissed at me about." Angelo waved at someone across the room, grinning as though his teeth were on review.

"Let's face it, Angelo, you've never had any use for him," Dan said, lowering his voice. "Why the hell you didn't go for a paternity test right off the bat like I suggested still escapes me."

"Christ, I can't believe you're bringing that up again. You know damn well why," Angelo said, slathering butter on a roll. "At the time, I was just moving ahead in politics, and how would it look if I couldn't keep the little woman down on the farm—barefoot, so to speak. Besides," Angelo added, "after what he did, I'm feeling kind of proud of the boy."

"Well, that's the biggest news of the day. After all, he *is* the only kid you're gonna get, legit or no." Dan had been having this discussion with Angelo since shortly after Tony was born and by now he was damn sick of it.

"Anyway, he's after detective status and wants Bernie to be his assistant. He's been bugging me for weeks."

"We'll see," Angelo replied. "Maybe he's ready, but for now, keep them in uniform."

"Well, we gotta use a little psychology here. Tony's riding pretty high right now, plus, we'll need him when Sheffield takes Nordblum to the Grand Jury. Tony'll have to testify. Maybe Bernie, too."

"I couldn't agree more," Angelo said good-naturedly, "but you still need to keep an eye on them. Here comes our lunch. I'm starved."

* * *

That afternoon, Angelo was startled out of a power nap at his desk when the intercom buzzed and Shirley told him that Tony was on his way in.

"His Honor," was all he said, dropping into a chair opposite his father.

"What's the matter with you, boy?"

"Well, I don't like going over his head, but the chief has gone back on his word," Tony said plaintively. "He promised that Bernie and I would be detectives if we got the shooter for him. And we did." Leaning forward in his chair, he picked up the ornate brass combination clock and barometer that had been on his father's desk since he was a kid, and at the same time knocked over a framed picture of his mother when he set it back down. Bending to pick it up, he saw that his own picture was still sitting in the corner behind his father's chair.

"Dan did mention that," Angelo told Tony as he set his mother's photo back on its stand. "But we don't hand out promotions based on performance in just one case. You've got to be on your toes. Are you on your toes every minute, boy?" he added, grinning.

As long as Tony could remember, his father had gotten a kick out of needling him.

"Come on, Pop, would you please take me seriously for a change," he said. "I can't stand working the beat. The chief promised me and I promised Bernie."

He knew he was really pushing the envelope, but this was important.

"I don't like to second-guess Dan," his father told him. "You know that, Tony, and I really don't like you asking me to. And how many times do I have to tell you not to call me Pop in the office?"

Tony leapt from his chair and, placing his fists in the middle of his father's desk, he thrust his face inches away from his father's. "When are *you* going to stop calling me *boy*?" he demanded. "Why do you hate me so much? What did I ever do to you, besides being born? Didn't you want a son, *His Honor*? Is that it?"

Hot tears suddenly brimmed in Tony's eyes. He fisted them away much as a child would have done.

Angelo struggled to his feet, probably hoping that Shirley hadn't overheard his outburst. He flexed his knees to free the cloth of his pants from his crotch, walked around the desk, and put one arm around Tony's shoulder. "You're just heated up over this promotion thing," he said, sounding more like a mayor than usual. "We'll try to work something out."

Tony shrugged his arm away. "Don't touch me, you phony," he muttered.

"How dare you . . .?"

"I dare because I don't care anymore." Tony told him. And then, turning his back on his father, he stalked out of the office, determined never to ask him for another thing.

* * *

Tony sat for a long time in the cruiser in the municipal parking lot. After a lifetime of struggling for his father's love, he had come to the unbearable truth that nothing he could do or say would ever be enough. Of course, he could move to another town where nobody had ever heard of *His Honor, Angelo Deluca*, and start right off as a detective, but he knew that wasn't about to happen. Not now. Not yet. Looking up at the window of his father's office, he imagined he saw him staring down at him and wondered if he ever regretted anything he did or said. A pigeon leapt winglessly from the edge of the roof, only spreading its wings at the last minute.

Shirley was just coming out of the building. She was shorter and much plumper than his mom. Younger, too. She had always been nice to him and Tony didn't mind that Pop had a thing going with her—he must be lonely since Mom died. Tony thought that he could really care about Shirley if he had a chance. She would never replace his mother, but he sure as hell wouldn't mind being included in holidays or even Sunday dinners at her house. He knew that if it was up to her, he would be invited, and Tony couldn't imagine what reason Pop gave her for not wanting his son to be included. The little angel he had snatched from the tree Shirley had been decorating peeked out from behind the car's visor. Tony felt a wave of embarrassment at having acted so childishly and decided to sneak it into the box of Christmas stuff in the basement. His father wouldn't notice and he was sure that Shirley would understand.

Tony took a deep breath and slowly let it go. For now, he just needed to deal with Bernie and his veiled threats about stretching the truth.

As a cop, it was depressing when you heard the excuses people came up with to justify lying to save their skin. There was Nordblum out there right now, probably going to church on Sundays, playing ball in the yard with his kids after work, telling himself that he was innocent.

His own situation wasn't like that at all, Tony told himself. So he'd changed from three to four witnesses. So what? He'd told Bernie it was a one-time thing, and it was. His intention had always been to play by the book, to be an honest cop. It's just that he was *sure* Nordblum was guilty and if that was true, he wasn't about to let him get off on any stupid technicalities.

He had reminded Bernie over and over that guilty was guilty no matter how you cut it. Nordblum was their man and they had had to make that affidavit confirm it.

Bernie was afraid of his own shadow—like when they were age fourteen and he wouldn't go off the rope swing at the lake until Tony swung out on it with him. He'd always trusted Tony before, and he should now.

Tony hoped he didn't have something up his sleeve—like telling how he had squeezed the ID out of that salesgirl in Parkdale. That's all he needed was for Chief to get wind of that, never mind His Honor. But maybe that's what Pop had meant when he'd said, no matter what.

The afternoon was slipping toward evening, he had less than an hour before the light would fade, and he needed to get back to the station.

* * *

Angelo stared down at the squad car sitting in the lot and wondered if Tony's anger might not be a wake-up call. It was true that he had never given the kid credit for much of anything. Maybe he should let up on him, tell Dan to go ahead and let him be a detective.

Way back, after they both had digressed and forgiven each other, Agnes had announced her pregnancy and Angelo had felt elated. The timing was so close that Tony *could* have been his child. But shortly after he was born, Angelo had this weird feeling that he wasn't the father, and he became more convinced of it as the kid developed—not the least bit athletic, blond instead of dark brown hair, a momma's boy—Angelo knew that his suspicions had grown way out of control, but he couldn't seem to stop.

Dropping back into his desk chair, he re-lit the Havana that had been resting in his ashtray. Blowing the smoke up toward the ceiling, he remembered the good times with Agnes, and the not-so-good. Except for that period, they'd had a great marriage right up until the end. Thinking on it, Angelo knew that his big regret was how disappointed she had been in the way he was with Tony. Being a public figure, he had kept his suspicions to himself, although, until the day she died, Agnes swore that Tony was his.

How ridiculous he had been; even if Tony wasn't his boy, everyone thought he was, and given how important public opinion was to him, that should have been enough. Was he jealous of his son? Afraid he might turn out to be better than he was?

Jesus, what kind of a man was he?

He stared at the beige carpet, which had been vacuumed to within an inch of its life and saw his footprints. Tony might be able to fill them after all.

Perhaps he should get that DNA test Dan kept bugging him about. It would be easy enough in today's world just to get a hair off Tony's uniform or take a coffee cup after he was done with it. Turning his swivel chair toward the window, Angelo looked across the field to where last year's cattails stood at the edge of a stream like quenched torches, and where, beyond, smoke curled seductively from a distant chimney. From somewhere deep within him came the nagging thought: Who could he pass the fruits of his lifetime of achievement on to, if not to a son? And now he knew, it had to be Tony or nobody.

* * *

Tony looked around the Legion Hall. So this is what he'd been missing. Most of the dignitaries he knew by name as parents of kids he grew up with, but some were strangers.

"Hello, Son," Angelo boomed from across the room. "Come on over here and meet a few of the constituents of this wonderful town of ours."

When his father put his arm around his shoulders, Tony felt like breaking into tears. How he had yearned for that touch, that casual acceptance as a boy. Now, it was almost more than he could bear.

"His Honor is certainly proud of you," one man said to Tony.

"We're so glad it wasn't you who got shot," another commented.

People crowded around him, congratulating him, telling His Honor how lucky he was to have such a son and Tony was thrilled when His Honor nodded in agreement.

Tony thought again of how their relationship had changed since the day of the 'sting' at Gordon's, how it had catapulted onto a totally different level. This was the third event he had attended at Pop's side. He was amazed at the number of people that fawned over his father, and how, now, they were showing *him* the same adulation. It was as though they hadn't known that he even existed before Pop brought him into the limelight. But, that's all changed now. Actually, this new rush of attention was a little overwhelming, but he'd take it in stride. All his life it's what he wanted.

"He's doing quite a job for Radcliff," Angelo was saying to someone while he beamed at Tony. "His mother, may she rest in peace, would be proud, too."

Tony gave the little speech that he had practiced over and over, that people had to give credit to the entire police force, not just him.

"Yes, sir," one familiar-looking man said, "His Honor told us how you handled the shooting and we citizens appreciate that. No back-up, you just got the job done. There are a lot of bad guys out there, you know—murderers, cheaters, liars—we need more fellows like you coming up through the ranks."

Holding himself very still, Tony listened, but all he heard was, *liar*. The air in the room seemed suddenly thin, insubstantial, and it was a conscious effort to breathe. Shame jumped in his gut. But shame was something he could not afford. Not now. Not ever.

* * *

CHAPTER TWENTY-FOUR

Eric found himself traversing the immense blue gully of depression. When he had finally admitted to losing his job, Shelly had immediately put in for full-time at the library, something the trustees had been after her to do for a long time. For almost fifteen years, Eric knew that her life had been contained within his, like the Russian nesting dolls, in a cocoon of domesticity. He had liked her dependency, it made him feel essential, needed. Now evidently she was enjoying the freedom to make her own decisions, to come and go as she pleased.

Shelly had insisted that Eric collect unemployment even though it was so damned humiliating. He began to sleep day and night between sweating fits and panic attacks, sometimes nine hours at a stretch. He went out for walks at midnight. When the boys came home from school, they found him sitting in a recliner in front of the television with the sound turned off, a Stouffer's frozen dinner untouched on a TV tray next to him. And all the while bitterness built inside him. When he could think of nothing else to do, he went out to the car and sat there with the keys in his hand, staring through the windshield at shadows that hung like phantoms amid the trees along the driveway. Sometimes he'd start the car, let it idle awhile before switching it off.

It became painfully clear that there was more to belonging somewhere than just being there, but where could he go without sinking, leaving no trace? One night, Eric had tried to take Shelly's hand in a hopeful moment, but he could see that her eyes were glassy green and blank as winter ice. Only then did he finally realize that it was merely the armature of habit that held them together. That, and pity. He had drawn his hand away like fingers turning loose from the side of a boat. Later that night, he had sat on the floor of the downstairs bathroom, for hours, holding in that same hand the Xanex pills that his doctor had prescribed for anxiety.

Eric then had retreated to the kitchen and knocked back four shots of scotch in quick succession, thinking it could relieve his depression. Later, waiting for the soft hammer of alcohol to send him reeling into sleep, he had lain beside Shelly listening to the thickness of her breath and thinking about how the evening's failure was part of a much larger one, and that his outrage was the price of his timidity; that, and his belief in the inherent goodness of mankind. Why, why, why had he ever let those cops into his apartment? This entire journey through hell had begun that day. Why hadn't he told them to get out? *Get the fuck out.* There was no law that said he'd had to talk to them. Why in the name of God hadn't he acted like a man?

He found himself wishing that he could commit some act that would put an end to all of this once and for all. Something that would forever close the way back to what his life had been, something violent, perhaps murder.

* * *

Mid-morning, when the phone rang, he let it go to message, only picking it up when he heard Maggie's voice.

"Hi, how's it going?"

"It's great. You're great. I'm great," he said as though he were conjugating a verb, in a voice that even he didn't recognize.

"I just wanted to tell you that you are missed around here."

"I am missed there," he repeated, emphasizing each word.

"You sure sound down in the dumps," she said, "and I can't blame you. No one can."

Eric didn't answer. He was watching a fly strut along the windowsill.

"Nobody here believes that you had anything to do with robbing those Gordon's stores, Eric."

"That'll do me a lot of good."

"My dad used to tell me that when everything seemed to be falling apart, I should pick myself up by my bootstraps and get going, because no one else was going to do it for you. So I'm telling you to do the same."

It was, Eric knew, good advice, but he found that somehow he couldn't respond. He wondered if, well-meaning as she was, Maggie knew just how down he was.

"Well anyway, think about that," Maggie told him. "You're a good person, Eric. Take care now. Bye."

After she hung up, he stood for a long time, just holding the receiver tight, as though it might keep him connected to her. Then, deciding he needed some fresh air, he pulled on an old pair of jeans and a black windbreaker over his pajama top and left his house, walking up one street and down another, thinking about what Maggie had said. And he did feel better, that is, until he turned a corner and saw people milling around in front of his house and a van with NBC written across the side.

"The press!" he cried out loud. Doubling back, he cut across a neighbor's front lawn. But it was too late. He'd been spotted. One tall, heavily made up, blonde reporter who he thought he recognized from Channel 12, came running along beside him, stretching her microphone in his face like a python.

"Can you give us a statement?"

"I'm innocent! I'm innocent."

The terror of it all nearly overcame him. Finally reaching his lawn, he flung himself onto the front porch and into the darkened house. Slamming the door, he locked it, safe at last among the clutter of boots and shoes.

"My God," he gasped out loud, "the vultures have come all the way from New York."

Still sitting on the floor, Eric recalled that Attorney Rothberg had warned him not to confide in anybody about what was happening; not family, friends, or even the boys. What a joke, he thought, listening to the hubbub outside his door.

Christ, why not talk about the accusations and the arrest; everyone else is.

When the boys came home from school, they now skirted whichever room he was in and Eric didn't need to be told that it was because they couldn't comprehend or deal with his depression. They were angry that kids at school were asking if what the newspapers said was true, and he couldn't blame them. They'd stopped asking him to come to their basketball games, and since Eric had completely lost his appetite, Jason and Arthur ate their meals alone with their mother.

* * *

Shelly had been avoiding her sister for months. But the day after Eric had told her what had happened with the press, she went over after work to see Robin, who met her at the door with open arms. Breaking into tears, Shelly blurted out an account of everything that had happened since Robin had gone with her to pay Eric's bail in three states.

"It's over," Shelly wailed on her sister's shoulder. "We're so completely finished. I don't know what to do. How can I ask him to leave when he's down and out? You should see him, Rob. You wouldn't recognize him. He sleeps all day, he's paranoid about talking to anybody, and he won't even answer the phone—especially when it's me."

"I want you to sit down," Robin said, pushing her into a kitchen chair before filling a kettle and putting it on the stove.

"It's as though the boys don't even exist anymore . . ." Shelly said, attempting to hold back fresh sobs.

"Look, Shel," Robin said firmly, "nobody's going to give you hero points for drowning along with the victim. You need to get on with your life. Eric's turned into a loser. And then there's another thing. Has it ever occurred to you that he might be guilty?"

Shelly jumped to her feet so suddenly that her chair flew backwards. "Robin, for God's sake, how could you believe he would do such a thing? Shoot a man? Steal diamond rings? Oh, it's no use talking about it," she added, struggling back into her coat. "I've got to get home and feed the boys. Eric doesn't even eat with us anymore."

"I'm so sorry, Shelly, I shouldn't have said that." Robin tried to stop her from leaving.

"Oh, I forgive you. It's the same thing everyone must be thinking. *My God, sometimes I'm even thinking it.* I shouldn't have come here. I just needed . . ."

And bursting into tears again, Shelly rushed out the door just as the teakettle began to whistle.

✳ ✳ ✳

"You've got to look for another job, Eric," Shelly told him.

"What could I possibly do, now?" Eric demanded, rubbing the stubble on his face. "I'm almost forty. My government clearance has been withdrawn. *For life.* Did you hear me, Shelly? For life. Even when or if I'm exonerated, I can never get that rating back. Don't you understand? I don't have a profession anymore."

But Shelly wasn't going to be put off that easily. "You could get a job selling office equipment. It would be a total career change, yet you'd still be in a related field." Turning her back on him, she started rinsing the dishes that were stacked in the sink. "No rumors would follow you from your former work community. It wouldn't require clearance of any kind and you already know so much about what computers can do. . . ." Her voice ran down like an old alarm clock that needed rewinding.

Eric sank back against the refrigerator and stared at her when she turned around. She looked exhausted.

"I just need to go to bed." She kept glancing up at the kitchen clock like she wanted permission to leave the room.

Finally, Eric realized that something fundamental had changed between them. She was trying to throw him a lifeline because she needed to be sure that he could function on his own before she cut him loose.

"Yes," he conceded in a flat voice, "I could do that."

"Good," she said, clearly relieved. "You can go to a headhunter tomorrow or check the morning paper. Good luck, Eric. You deserve it," she added.

He tried to smile reassuringly but he felt as though she had just handed him a death sentence, which, in a way, she had.

✽ ✽ ✽

CHAPTER TWENTY-FIVE

The next day, Attorney Rothberg's assistant called Eric to tell him that his witnesses were not being cooperative. "Maybe they're trying to distance themselves from you by not being forthcoming," she told him, "but whatever their reason, it doesn't look good for establishing your whereabouts the day of the shooting in Radcliff."

"I can't believe this." He closed his eyes and bars of fire darted across his eyelids. He didn't think he could take any more rejection.

"Mr. Rothberg wants you to tell your former colleagues and customers what's going on and that you need them to back up your alibi."

"One minute I'm not to talk, the next minute you want me to ask them for help."

"But we *are* making progress, Mr. Nordblum."

Was it just ordinary bad luck, Eric wondered, or was the devil at work here? Whatever did he do to deserve this? No one close to him seemed to understand, no colleague had come forward to back him up, except, of course, Maggie.

"Try not to be discouraged," Rothberg's assistant continued as if by rote. "It's the function of the Grand Jury to protect the innocent from hasty and malicious prosecutions. It has always stood as a check to ensure that a charge was founded on sufficient and competent evidence."

"Yeah, I really believe that."

"Don't forget what Alfred Hitchcock said: 'An innocent man has nothing to fear . . .' or something like that," she concluded with a self-conscious giggle.

"Jesus!" was all Eric could think of to say before hanging up. Dim and translucent, his reflection in the window over the kitchen sink stared back at him while the shadow of a long twisted cobweb, caught on the eaves outside, swung back and forth across his face like a noose.

Now, before he could even think about job hunting, he'd have to force himself to contact everyone that had spoken to him or seen him that fateful day, November 29th, and report back to Rothberg. But he had to face the fact that privacy was no longer an issue. He'd do it for the boys because, for him, there was nothing else left to live for.

Without thinking it through, Eric sat down at his desk and called Rothberg's assistant back. "I was wondering if you have the name of the salesclerk who identified me in Parkdale," he said.

"I'm not sure I'm supposed to give out that kind of information in a case, Mr. Nordblum."

"Why in Christ's name not? I *am* the case. It's about me, remember? I'm the accused and your boss is my attorney. Now, get me that goddamn name."

He wouldn't take this shit lying down, he told himself. Not anymore. He had nothing left to lose and he'd go to hell before he would leave this legacy of total failure to his sons.

* * *

Wednesday morning, while Shelly was getting dressed for work, Eric mumbled from under the covers that he'd like her to take the bus to work and when she asked why, he didn't answer.

"Oh yes, those cops took the Pontiac *and* searched the house for a gun. A gun, for God's sake, Eric, a gun." She went downstairs.

Right after he heard her slam the front door, Eric jumped out of bed, showered and shaved for the first time in weeks. Dressing carefully in a go-to-the-office outfit, he polished his shoes, and went down to the kitchen for a cup of coffee. The pot was empty, so he made some instant in a travel cup and left the house by nine-thirty in the BMW. Checking a map, he plotted the route to Parkdale. It was just before the Delaware River. Later, he hardly remembered the ride except that it started to rain and the windshield wipers were slapping out their steady beat. All he could think of was that he had to do *something* to prove his innocence.

In Parkdale, Eric stopped to ask directions to Gordon's and was sent to a mall only two miles ahead. Once in the store, he walked up to the closest jewelry counter and asked for Mary Fletcher and was directed to fine jewelry.

Eric stood back a moment, watching the girl that had been pointed out to him. She seemed like an ordinary sort, dressed nicely and smiling engagingly at the woman she was waiting on. Certainly she didn't look like someone who would lie. Eric waited till the customer left, not even sure what he was going to do.

"Hi. I'm here to look at an engagement ring," he said.

"Oh, yes, I can certainly help you," Mary told him earnestly. "We have a wide range to choose from."

She reached under the counter, pulling out a tray of assorted diamond rings. Eric noticed that she kept her hand on the tray when he picked up a ring. He held it up between them so she had to look straight at him.

"Say, have we met before?" He made it a sucker-punch question out of the blue.

"What?"

"I'm asking you if we know each other. Somehow I think I've seen you somewhere."

"No, I don't believe I've seen you before, but I have so many customers coming and going, probably everyone seems a little familiar."

Eric noticed how quickly she put the tray away. Was it possible that she actually thought that he might snatch one of the rings and take off with it? Certainly her mood had changed. She stood, arms crossed, eyeing him warily.

"So do I look familiar or not?" Now she was looking across the aisle at another jewelry counter. There was a man there but his back was turned. "Look at my *face*. Is it the least bit familiar to you?" Eric knew he was starting to lose it.

"No. And if you don't stop, I'm going to call security. Please, just leave."

Eric reached across the counter and grabbed her arm. "You told the police that I robbed you. For God's sake, you just said that you've never seen me before. What's your game? Why are you doing this to me?"

She wrenched her arm free and pressed both hands over her eyes. She was not making a sound but Eric was sure she was sobbing. He turned and walked swiftly toward the exit.

He didn't care how long he had to wait in the parking lot; he wasn't leaving until he got a confession out of her.

* * *

CHAPTER TWENTY-SIX

Chief Fortini was thinking about Donna Sheffield. Although she was sexy and considerably younger than he, she was, he guessed, past the point of hoping to be a mother. He'd never wanted a kid and just to be sure, he hadn't married. But at this point, he wouldn't mind having someone to eat with, and talk about police matters. And it would be a good thing if he could get some regular tail, all right under his own roof. Being police chief made him feel as though he was always on display, always out there for people to criticize or hold up to their kids as an example to live up to. There never was time for him to be off-stage. He had no damn private life and could really picture getting something going with Donna.

She had only been appointed prosecutor ten months ago and he wasn't sure how to get things rolling, but he figured it would be a good start if he ran over to Dunkin' for some coffee and donuts to take upstairs in the next day or two. He'd be real casual . . . Yeah, that was the way to go about it. Coffee and donuts had always opened doors for him.

* * *

On Thursday, Chad Richardson called the Radcliff Police Department and asked for Chief Fortini. "So, I finally reached you," he barked as soon as Dan picked up. "It's been weeks since the last follow-up on the shooting. What the hell is going on with you?"

Oh, Christ, he'd meant to call him.

"Now, hold on a minute," Dan said, stalling while he searched his desk for the Gordon's folder. "Who is this?"

"I'm the temporary manager at Gordon's," Chad said, adding his name, "where the *shooting* occurred, in case you have forgotten; where your incompetent cop let the bastards get away, where I have to stay until the robbery is solved. I'm the person who signed off on suing the goddamn town of Radcliff. Does that jog your memory?"

"Of course I know who you are and I'd like to say once again that the town of Radcliff is grateful that you didn't sue, we . . ."

"Believe me, that wasn't my decision," he told him. "Right now, I'm a citizen requesting service from the town where this business pays mega taxes."

"How is your injury doing?"

"I still need a cane and my leg still hurts."

"I'm really sorry to hear that, Mr. Richardson."

"Don't change the goddamn subject."

"Actually, I was just planning to update you today."

"Oh, really."

"Thanks to the description by you and other witnesses, a composite was created and circulated which has led to the arrest of the shooter," he said, ignoring his attitude. "Probably the leader. I'm surprised you didn't read about it in *The Radcliff Record* or *The Tribune.*"

"Why would I ever be interested in reading local papers, other than to check Gordon's ads?"

"Well, how about the *New York Daily News?* The arrest was written up in that, too." Dan couldn't help but brag even though it hadn't made the front page.

"Maybe you don't know that Radcliff doesn't carry *The News,* not even the Sunday edition. And what the hell are we talking about newspapers for?"

"In any case," Dan continued, "Officer Deluca found this fugitive single-handedly."

"Good. Now maybe I can get out of this backwater town."

Not a word of thanks, Dan thought; no gratitude for prompt police work.

"So, how did your genius make a positive I.D. without talking to me?" Chad continued. "Don't tell me he remembered everything I said that infamous day?"

"Of course not. Tony and his assistant, Bernie Pigeon, interviewed you and the witnesses at the store, only a few days afterwards."

"I hate to burst your bubble, Fortini, but neither Deluca nor his sidekick ever came back to the store to talk to me. That's why I have left all those *unanswered* messages for you."

"That's not so, sir. Officer Deluca stated in his report that he spoke to the witnesses in Radcliff and . . ."

"Okay, whatever," Chad broke in impatiently, "I don't give a shit about what he said as long as you have made an arrest. I don't suppose the ring was recovered by your star cop."

"No, sir. Unfortunately."

"Of course not. Have you found the other two? How long before this guy is convicted?"

"We're going to Grand Jury on June 12th."

"Hell, that's a couple of months away. Will I have to testify?"

"Yup. You're the main witness in New Jersey. Don't worry. If you're back in New York by then, just give us your address and we'll let you know."

"Yeah, just like you've been keeping me informed all along . . ."

"You don't need to get upset, sir, we're doing the best we can, but . . . ."

Dan was interrupted by the sound of Chad hanging up. What a bastard, he thought, saying he wasn't interviewed. Tony had had two positive witnesses there and Chad *had* to have been one of them. And with that, Dan pushed a tincture of doubt into the farthest reaches of his mind.

* * *

"Tell Tony I want to see him, now," Dan bellowed at his secretary through his office doorway. While he waited, he popped a Tums in his mouth, followed by a swallow of cold black coffee.

Among other things that had gone wrong lately, his coffee and donut idea had fallen flat. Donna Sheffield didn't eat between meals and *never* ate donuts. Maybe he should just ask her out to dinner. Someplace special, like one of those high-class restaurants in Patterson. He was just looking through the yellow pages when Tony came sauntering into his office.

"Where's your uniform, Deluca?" he demanded.

"These are my detective duds, Chief," Tony said. "Check out the quality of this leather." He offered his sleeve for Dan to feel.

"What are you, crazy?" the chief asked him scornfully. "The minute we're finished here I want you to dump that outfit and put your uniform on."

"But Chief, you said if I cracked this case, you would promote me to detective." Tony's disappointment filled the air like a bad smell.

"I never said any such thing and the case isn't cracked until Nordblum gives up his accomplices, we find the gun, and all three are convicted," Dan told him, absentmindedly slamming the telephone book shut. "Now, what I called you in here for was this folder. Where the hell are the notes on your original interview with Nordblum?" There was more than just an undertone of threat built into his question.

"I was doing the talking, Chief. Bernie was supposed to be taking notes. I'll go get them from him."

"Don't interrupt me, I'm not finished. Where are the reports of the actual arrests in Tolleson and Radcliff? Where are the copies of the arrest warrants? Where are the statements from the witnesses? Where are the reports from other precincts?" Suddenly Dan was on his feet with his face inches away from Tony's. "There's no evidence of a case in this folder," he said, whapping Tony over the head with it.

"But Chief . . ."

"No buts about it. Don't you realize that the prosecutor is asking me for this information and I won't be able to give her shit? Get back to your office and don't come out until I have all the info on this case, *in writing,* on my desk. No time out for eating or pissing. If I see you in the lunchroom before you're finished, I'll . . ."

When the Chief raised his fist threateningly, the look on Tony's face was a study in sheer terror.

* * *

Tony turned and ran out of Dan's office to the lunchroom. "Bernie, quick, grab that box of muffins and some Cokes and follow me. Hurry."

Stopping at his locker, he carefully hung up his leather jacket and jeans and angrily pushed his feet into the legs of his uniform, shoes and all.

Bernie was waiting for Tony in the cubicle they shared. "What's your problem, detective?" he demanded with a big shit-eating grin.

"Shut up about detective. The chief just reamed me out because there weren't enough notes in the Gordon's folder. Christ, he wants us to write down every little friggin' thing that's happened."

"Shit," Bernie exclaimed. "I warned you we should've been taking notes all along. But no, you kept telling me it wasn't necessary—that we could reconstruct conversations afterward. But we didn't. And now I doubt if we can." He covered his face with his thin, bony hands. "Oh, God, what's going to happen?"

"Quit your whining. We can do it now. Come on, get your pad. You write, I'll dictate. We both have *some* notes—we can work from them."

Reaching for the largest muffin in the box, Tony handed another one to Bernie, who ate it in three bites and washed it down with a Coke.

How unfair is that? Tony thought. He never gains a pound.

"And make your writing look different with each report," Tony added, looking over Bernie's shoulder.

"This better work," Bernie warned, "because I'm not going down with you, Tony."

Ignoring the warning, Tony paced around their desk as he dictated while Bernie wrote furiously. Suddenly, Tony stopped in front of his mail basket. Jesus H. Christ. He couldn't believe his eyes. Right there on top was a memo addressed to him from Avondale, Arizona reporting that, on March 14th, three jewelry bandits hit Merwin's jewelry store, getting away with a diamond ring valued at ten thousand dollars. A diamond ring. The same MO. Three perps. *Three.*

He pulled the report out of the basket and folded it in half and then in half again, running his thumbnail along the crease until the square of paper lay flat in his hand. He stared at it as though it would send him a message, telling him what to do, before stuffing it inside his shirt.

Tony felt like he was in free fall. Shuffling through the papers on his desk, he pulled out the report from the tail he had put on Eric and ran his finger down the dates to March 14th—*sleeping in his car in Wal-Mart parking lot.*

"What the hell are you dreaming about, Tony?" Bernie rubbed his writing hand and slouched back in the chair, stretching his long legs out in front of him. "I'm finished doing these reports, but you can bet your ass I'm not the one whose gonna sign them."

"Yeah, all right. I gotta go. I'll be back in less than an hour."

"Where?"

"Out."

"Want company?"

Without bothering to answer, Tony rushed through the squad room and out to his cruiser.

Shit, shit, shit. They must be wrong. I know what I saw—Eric Nordblum aiming that gun at me and driving the getaway car. The gray Pontiac.

* * *

Later that afternoon, Tony drove his squad car slowly back to the station. The day was bright and windy, a film of delicate white clouds scuttling eastward. It wasn't in his nature to cheat, he thought, but he was terrified. The treachery of what he had just done opened before him like a deep well he dared not peer into. It had been easy enough to drop a few 9 mm bullets under the seat of Nordblum's impounded car, soon to be discovered by someone. If he had stuck with the usual bureaucracy and hadn't done *something* to back his story, Nordblum would go free, and with *his* freedom would come his own demise. So, he had to do it—*no matter what.*

He cursed the day he ever met Eric Nordblum, the wimp. Why hadn't he just thrown them out of his apartment? Tony wished to Christ that he had. Even then, there had been that nagging voice, telling him that not all the evidence lined up, but had he listened? Hoping for glory, he had blundered along, exaggerating a little here, stretching the truth there, littering his path with irrevocable lies. The distant glitter of everything that was possible in the world, things he had wanted for himself, now felt unattainable, like climbing a mountain that rose into the clouds and had no top and no end.

Picking up his cell phone, he saw that there was a message from His Honor: *Shirley wants you to come around noon for Sunday dinner and be sure to reserve Thursday at seven for Candidates' Night. A man should have his son beside him.*

Tony cringed. Finally, finally, this was what he had dreamed of and the tide of his actions was coming to take it away. He needed to hold on to his original suspicions, put everything else aside. He felt, still with some certainty, that Nordblum was guilty, and if he had to cut a few corners to nail the poor bastard, it was okay. He thought poor bastard, because if he wasn't the shooter, then Tony might have wrecked his life. Not to mention his own.

He decided that this situation he was in was best looked at in tiny glimpses. When you build one big nasty lie on a series of little ones, you had to build it strong and solid. Because it was usually the simple truth that undid you.

Passing Chester Street, he noticed that the maples in front of his apartment house had started to bud with the delicate green shades of early April and he made a mental note to buy flowers for his mother's grave.

Back at the station, Tony picked up the folder, now full of everything to do with the case against Nordblum. Even though Bernie had written down everything Tony had told him to, in the end he had flat-out refused to sign the reports, so Tony put his signature on all of them. Slipping quietly into the chief's office, he shoved it under a pile of other folders on his desk.

He had put his finger in the dike, he told himself, but even so, that might not be enough.

✻ ✻ ✻

CHAPTER TWENTY-SEVEN

"These notes are barely legible," Donna told Dan, "but it does seem that we have more than enough fodder with the four positive witnesses for the Grand Jury to indict Nordblum. I wish you guys could find the accomplices or some hard evidence. That would cinch it for me."

"There's not a damn piece of evidence on the other two," he said, "but I'm guessing that Nordblum will eventually give them up."

Dan watched her rummage through her purse for her ChapStick and smear it on her lips. "I hear from Nordblum's new attorney that he's got an alibi," she said. "Do you know who the new attorney is?"

"I couldn't even begin to guess."

"David Rothberg, right out of a high-powered office in Manhattan."

"No kidding? I guess Nordblum is forking out some of his drug money."

"Now that you mention it, I was wondering where the drugs come into this jewelry scam? Was any evidence found on him or in his apartment? I mean, where did Tony come up with the drug idea?"

"I'm not exactly sure, but you can bet I'll find out for you." Dan started for the door before adding, as if it were an afterthought; "Uh, Donna, I was wondering if you'd like to go over to Patterson for dinner some evening. You know, I mean get kinda dressed up and go out."

"Oh, gee, Dan, I thought you knew," she said, sounding genuinely surprised. "I'm seeing Robert Hazelton over in the Attorney General's office. As a matter of fact, we live together."

As she averted her eyes, the black marble antique clock that sat on her bookcase struck ten. The clock was a gift from her grandmother—that's what she had told him last year when he had helped her move into her office.

"Uh, no," Dan stammered, "actually, I didn't know that, but . . ."

He cleared his throat, unable to continue. All he could think of was when he'd asked Amanda Wight to the senior prom, she had insisted that he ask her parents who, believe it or not, had said no, claiming she was too young or some ridiculous excuse. Afraid to say that he was from the wrong side of the tracks.

"I'd rather not start anything," Donna continued blithely. "You understand where I'm coming from, don't you? No hard feelings?"

"Sure," he said as if he meant it.

"Good," she said as if she believed it.

He could feel his face burning. All this time she had been living with someone. And not just someone, but Hazelton from the Attorney General's office.

"Okay," she said, rising. It was a dismissal if there ever was one.

"I've got to start setting up appointments with all these witnesses," she added briskly, all business now. "There's going to be a helluva lot of statements to take."

She needn't bother trying to soften the insult, he thought. She can go to hell.

And then he was out the door, feeling as though he was struggling his way out from under a ton of bricks.

* * *

Dan stood at his office window watching Donna struggle with an armful of folders and a full briefcase as she picked her way through the parking lot. It had poured throughout the night, leaving large puddles of muddy water deep enough to top her shoes, and it was still raining. If things had turned out differently, he would have gone outside to give her a hand. But, not now. *Let Mr. Prick Hazelton look after her.*

Angelo had called Dan last night to tell about his sudden urge, after all these years, to go ahead with the DNA test. He had said it was finally time for him to know whether or not Tony was truly his son. With this in mind, he had asked Dan to get his hands on something Tony had touched and get it over to the lab. And, of course, to do it on the q.t. Even though Dan had urged his friend many times to find out once and for all, it now made him feel as though he were leaning on a knife's edge, uneasiness slicing into him. If Angelo had proof that he was Tony's father, would he then, in turn, accelerate his career? The thought of Tony actually becoming Chief of Police someday made him feel physically ill.

He reached from his desk chair to switch on his radio that sat on the windowsill, turning it low to a country-western station on which the songs told of overwhelming loneliness, which accompanied his own sadnesses, formless and self-consuming.

With his copy of the Nordblum folder in hand, Dan decided he would personally check *all* of Tony's findings, reports, witness statements—everything. Angelo would be making the mistake of his life if he was picturing Tony in any job other than a cop on the beat.

* * *

When the DNA results came in a few days later, Dan went straight to Angelo's office. He stared at his old friend a moment before reaching into his pocket and pulling out a plastic bag with an empty Coke can in it. Slamming it down hard on Angelo's desk, he removed the folded lab report from the inside pocket of his jacket.

"Here, *Pop*," he spoke softly, "congratulations. You're the proud father of a bouncing baby boy."

* * *

Angelo had been so stunned with the lab report Dan had given him that his blood had literally turned cold. The minute Dan left, he told Shirley to leave early.

"Are you all right?" she asked him. "What's going on with you? There's mystery in the air," she added, laughing.

Angelo nearly shoved her out the door. "I'm fine," he said. "You go on home. I just need to go over some personal matters."

So Tony was his son after all, his flesh and blood son.

He remembered, with terrible clarity, the tonal shifts and pulses of Tony's visit to his office weeks ago. Even their most recent connection couldn't erase the deep-seated pain of hearing over and over again the despair in his son's voice that day. Well, he had already started to repair their relationship, but now how he wished he had invited Tony to the christening of the Deluca Bridge; it would have made him feel important. And to the Governor's Ball. They could have rented tuxedos together. It would have been good for laughs. Why had he wanted all the notoriety for himself? Because he hadn't believed that Tony was his son? His real son? When Agnes had wanted to name their baby Angelo, he had forbidden it, and they had compromised with just the letter A as Tony's middle initial. *Maybe Tony would like to change it now, legally. He would go along with that.*

Angelo knew himself and the full depth of what he had become over the years. He was well acquainted with the serpent that lay coiled inside him—the searing ambition to win at any cost and most importantly, not to let anything shameful be connected to him.

The lab report lay in the middle of his desk. Angelo re-read it several times, and then he laid it flat, smoothing it neatly. Next to it sat the Coke can, the absolute evidence, still in the plastic bag. This would be a pivotal moment, he told himself; it was never too late to make a fresh beginning. He had already started.

Tomorrow, I'll invite him out to lunch. Not with Dan. Just us two. Detective Deluca and His Honor. He'll like that. And I'll definitely involve him in my campaign next fall. I'll have him sit up on the stage with me. My son, Anthony Angelo Deluca.

* * *

Later that same day, Dan caught Tony just as he was leaving the station. "Come into my office for a minute, would you?" he asked.

"Sure, Chief," Tony said cheerfully, putting a lid on any tension he might be feeling. "Want to come with me over to Sherman's? We could talk there."

Dan didn't bother to answer. "Sit down," he said bluntly, thumping his fist on the Nordblum folder. "What's this crap about two witnesses in Kensington, New York? Detective Fornier copied me on his report that he had only *one* witness. Why the hell did you put two in your report?"

Tony shrugged, cupping his head between his shoulder blades. His hands lay palm upward on his thighs and he sat watching them as if they had somehow unaccountably appeared. "It must just be a mistake, Chief," he said. "I'll have Bernie correct that right away." Getting to his feet, he started for the door. "As a matter of fact, I'll correct it myself, right now. I won't wait for Bernie. Okay?"

"What is Bernie, your personal secretary?" the Chief demanded. "Get back here and sit your ass down in that chair." He wagged his finger in Tony's face. "I'm letting you know *this* right now. If I find one more discrepancy in your reports, you're not only off the force, but you will never work in the field of law enforcement again. Is that clear?"

Dwarfed by the events that he had put into motion, Tony felt his muscles seize in terror. "Yes, sir," he said. "May I go now, Chief?"

"Get the hell out of here," Dan told him in no uncertain tones.

Dan made him feel rejected, like a dog from the pound when it dug up the yard. But he wasn't going to give up hope that he could pull this off. He just had to think smart, like His Honor did.

* * *

CHAPTER TWENTY-EIGHT

Eric kept calling his lawyer, only to find that each time his questions were answered by an assistant whose job it was to insulate her boss from tiresome clients with complaints. "Mr. Rothberg is taking alibi statements, Mr. Nordblum," she reported, "from everyone who could prove that you couldn't possibly have committed these crimes by testifying that you were elsewhere. Those were filed with the County Prosecutor's office in March."

"March?" Eric exclaimed, his tone between accusatory and pugnacious. "It's nearly the end of April and the Grand Jury date is June 12th. Have the alibi statements been coming in from that list I sent you?"

The early sun pierced the window in a fine, thin tube of light. He looked out at his yard where the daffodils had opened, fluttering like flights of goldfinches on their stems. Spring, his most favorite season, had arrived without notice.

"Yes, Mr. Nordblum, we're almost through with that phase of planning your defense. The problem is," she told him with a hint of disdain, "Radcliff is experiencing delays."

"What kind of delays?"

"Apparently, the City of Radcliff is debating with the Meriden county prosecutor as to who is responsible for paying police officers to go around to check your alibis."

"Are you telling me they haven't even started yet?" Eric snarled into the phone. "I'm going to call that Radcliff police chief and get to the bottom of this."

"No!" she responded quickly, "don't do that, please. It would be highly improper. All you have to do is be patient . . ."

"Patient? Do you realize my life is over? Do you realize that ever since last Thanksgiving everything has changed; that I'll never be able to go back to my old life? Never?"

Bitterness surged through Eric like an electric shock, made even worse by the fact that it was a reflection of someone's deliberate and reckless indifference toward him.

* * *

The negotiating between the City of Radcliff and the Meriden county prosecutor as to who would pay the overtime, the mileage, and the lunches for police officers to travel interstate to check Eric's alibis went on for another week until finally Judge Barrington stepped in with the directive for them to cut the expenses down the middle, and to do it fast because he would *not* allow the June 12th trial date to be continued.

* * *

Eric, who had a Masters in Electrical Engineering, a man who had had government clearance to work with military bases as an engineer, a man *who had had years of experience and a high salary,* decided to answer an ad for a sales rep in a new start-up tech company, a job that paid $36,000 a year, plus commission.

Was it possible that anyone went through life without contemplating the thin blue line of suicide? To give oneself over to death? And what was the distance you had to travel between the idea and the act when it comes in its most seductive guise as a resolution to exhausting and unsolvable events not of your doing?

Before setting up an interview, Eric called Maggie who agreed to pull his résumé from the files at MTS. She seemed really glad to hear from him, in spite of everything. In fact, she suggested that, instead of mailing the papers to him, they meet for lunch, thoughtfully naming a restaurant several miles this side of Dalton to be sure he wouldn't bump into anyone from his past.

Maggie was slim with an engaging smile and skin that had the scrubbed, healthy look of a woman who liked the outdoors. All during lunch, Eric was aware of her watching him, an uncritical regard, something no one else had shown him for a long time. But when she rested her hand on his, Eric pulled it back as though he had been burned.

"Don't do that."

"I'm so sorry. It didn't mean anything . . ."

"It's what started this whole mess in my life."

"That's not true, Eric. It was the arrest, not us."

"There *is* no us."

"I know that. Let's just drop it."

After that, she actually praised him for moving forward, reminding him that once this conspiracy was behind him, he could regain his stature in the workplace. And he noticed that she was careful to avoid shoptalk from MTS.

"Keep going," she told him, her words constituting an encouragement so tenuous he dared not test them with even a sigh, much less a question. And yet, her voice was steady and sure.

✿ ✿ ✿

CHAPTER TWENTY-NINE

On this beautiful May morning, Bernie and Tony carried on as usual, joking and laughing in their cubicle, although there was an edge on everything they did now, an uncertainty that had never been there before, making them like people who laugh at funerals. Because Bernie was suffering. Sometimes he felt that he couldn't bear another minute of not knowing where he stood in this mess. It was with terrifying resolve that he waited until Tony left before knocking on Dan's open door.

"Come in," Dan shouted, "and bring Tony with you." Bernie could see that he was bent over the reports he had written, *but not signed.*

The last good road open to Bernie now was confession, which he had decided was his only hope of absolution. "Tony left for lunch. But, Chief," he said before Dan could go on, his knees growing soft with fear, "I want to talk to you."

"Make it short, because I have a lot to say to you," Dan interrupted rudely, taking a sip of his coffee; his eyes looked like small brown marbles over the white rim of the cup.

With crippling remorse, Bernie launched into having been a silent witness to Tony's exaggerations and *actual lies* about Eric Nordblum. Before he was finished, Bernie was grasping his two fists together against his narrow chest.

Bernie didn't hold anything back. He added that the notes in the folder had been written long after the fact, complete with considerable embellishment. His words fell from his mouth into the darkest corners of the police chief's office.

Without saying a word, Dan stared into a space just beyond Bernie's left shoulder, obviously stupefied by shock. Finally, he made some horrible noise, like a bark.

"What about the witnesses?" he asked, narrowing his eyes ominously. "Were they all made up, too?"

"There was actually only one positive witness," Bernie told him, "from Kensington, the others were coerced . . ."

Suddenly Bernie stopped, his head cocked toward the outer office like a dog who's heard his master's whistle.

"Was that Tony's voice?" he whispered, his gaunt face etched with fear.

"I don't give a flying fuck," the chief told him. "You just keep talking."

Bernie got up and closed the door but stood with his hand still on the handle.

"That's all I can think of, Chief," he said. "I'm feeling really sick. I have to go to the head." He opened the door and then turned back to Dan. "Tony's not a really bad person; he does believe that Nordblum's guilty and he wants to please you and His Honor so badly, I . . . I think he just got carried away."

And then, vomit rising in his throat, he ran from the room.

* * *

When Bernie had come into his office, Dan had been reviewing all the unknowns in the case. He had been angry then and now his wrath was monumental. Picking up the phone, he dialed Angelo's private line.

"Get your fat ass over to O'Malley's and meet me in the back. Now." His voice reached through the phone line and slapped Angelo in the face.

Ten minutes later, they sat huddled at a table way in the back of the restaurant at three in the afternoon, the only patrons. When Dan finished repeating Bernie's accusations as well as adding his own suspicions, there was a long silence, as if both of them had forgotten their lines. Just thinking about what had happened—what was *going to happen,* fanned Dan's heartburn. He belched sourly.

"My head is on the block for this, Angelo," he said. "Ultimately, I'm responsible."

His Honor's stony silence sucked all of the oxygen out of the room. When he finally spoke, it was, Dan thought, almost a relief. "The value of a secret depends on who it must be kept from," Angelo said enigmatically.

"What the hell is that supposed to mean?"

"A secret that became part of the silence itself . . ."

Dan leaned toward Angelo, his eyes black pinpoints of fury. "Do you mean bluff it through or do you mean put the blame somewhere else?"

Angelo merely shrugged.

"Whatever we do, it has to be immediate. Today."

* * *

An edge of paper began to slide from the mouth of Donna's fax machine. *Another one.* That made two devastating confirmations, one after the other. The first one had been from the attorney from Kensington, New York and the second from Dalton, Connecticut. Both told her the same thing: the charges against Eric Nordblum had been dropped. It seemed that, when his alibi was checked, everyone concerned had vouched for Eric's whereabouts on November 29th. In the end, what it amounted to was that everything that Tony had told them had been proven false.

That left New Jersey, and Prosecutor Donna Sheffield, whose investigation of Eric's alibi had been held up by that ridiculous squabble of 'who would pay' holding the bag in Radcliff. As a result, her reports weren't in yet. You can bet your bippy she was prepared to light a fire under their infuriating butts. Wouldn't you know this was her first big case as prosecutor? She suspected that the egg on her face would be enough to make her into soufflé. And here she was, two weeks before the Grand Jury was to convene.

* * *

Later that same afternoon, Bernie sat facing Angelo and Dan in the mayor's office with the door closed. Dan knew the terrible moral wrongness of what they were proposing. However, after clearing his throat, he forced himself to continue.

"The bottom line is this," he said, "if you take responsibility for lying to the judge about the witnesses in the Nordblum case, we'll let you off with a reprimand and a two-week suspension. Then in six months, after you've attended intensive training, and things have cooled down, you'll be elevated officially to detective. That's a promise from the mayor and from me."

"But it wasn't me, Chief, it was Tony," Bernie told him, crossing himself and throwing a look toward Angelo. "He made me sign that damn affidavit." His weak excuse hung in the air like a loud fart.

"It's what you wanted, Bernie. Detective."

"I don't know what you mean."

"I think you do," Angelo said sternly, his oversized chest rising and falling heavily. He glanced up at the photo of Reagan on the wall and closed his eyes.

He had told Dan that he didn't want Tony's name connected with this case in any way, especially not now, knowing what he knew, and they had both agreed that Bernie was the perfect fall guy. Dan knew it wouldn't take much to convince him to take full responsibility, which would keep Tony's name from being tarnished, not to mention his own and Angelo's.

"This isn't fair," Bernie whined, squirming in his chair. "Tony should be here, too."

"Never mind about Tony," Angelo told him angrily, "we'll deal with him later."

"Jesus H. Christ, Bernie," Dan broke in, his voice rising out of control, "you two never looked at Nordblum's goddamn DayTimer. Even Colombo asks where people were on the night of the murder. You don't have to be Dick Tracy or Sherlock Holmes to know that that's the key question. But of all the things you guys did, the goddamn affidavit was the worst. It started this whole investigation and arrest."

There was a brief hostile silence.

"You lied to the judge," Dan added with a finality that carried its own threatening message.

Dan observed that he was trying to concentrate in order to think clearly when Bernie removed his glasses and rubbed his eyes. The kid had made so little of his life—yet he had always seemed to be yearning for things beyond his reach. Now, when Bernie nodded, Dan could see the surge of unruly hope that spread across his face. Was it possible that this pathetic, poor-excuse-for-a-cop didn't see the handwriting on the wall?

* * *

CHAPTER THIRTY

As Shelly approached the front door, Eric saw her pause on the sidewalk and look down, studying the spidery cracks in the cement as though she was preparing herself for something she didn't want to do. It was a moment of such private vulnerability that he stepped back from the window. After a motionless beat, Eric punched in the number he now knew by heart.

"More good news," Attorney Rothberg's assistant reported in response to Eric's inquiry. "New York and Connecticut have dropped the charges against you. Now we're just waiting for New Jersey. You're almost in the clear, Mr. Nordblum." She paused, probably waiting for him to say thank you or to praise her boss. *Well screw that. Screw them and all the money I've shelled out, lining their greedy pockets.*

He hung up the phone. "Was that Rothberg's office, again?" Shelly asked as she entered the front hall.

"Yes. It looks like the whole thing is crumbling. That's wonderful, isn't it? After how many months?" Eric saw Shelly recoil from the pain and humiliation he knew was mapped on his face.

"Over six," Shelly replied all too quickly. They looked at one another in silence, watching as the seconds passed. Her sigh hung in the air like an accusation.

"What will happen now?" he asked her. "I mean between us?"

"Well, I've been thinking," she said, twisting her hands over and over like a knitter without yarn, not making eye contact. "Now that everything is going to be okay, I think you should move out again."

Eric stumbled backwards as if she had struck him. "Okay?" he said. "What the hell do you mean *okay*? Our marriage? You? Certainly not me."

The words were hurled at her like a gob of spit.

"I can't talk to you when you're like this, Eric," she told him.

"Don't you turn your back on me, dammit!" he shouted. "Now is the perfect time to say what you want. Because life is good again. I'll get my job back. The boys won't be ashamed of me anymore. You'll love me again. Yeah, everything is really okay."

It was then that Eric began to weep, huge shoulder-thrusting sobs. Shelly stared at the floor, waiting for him to regain control.

"Eric, you know our life together as we lived it, is over," she began cautiously. "This whole travesty has been horrible for you, and for me and the boys, too. The only thing left for each of us is the future."

She placed one hand on his shoulder. Her touch made him feel like pleading, but he didn't.

"We need to follow separate paths, but you know we'll always be joined by our children," she continued. "They won't suffer from our mistakes as long as we don't allow it. We can make joint custody work."

On the tide of her words, he drew away from her, unable to respond. His reaction was a silence that drew everything else into it. Finally, he spoke. "Do whatever you want," he said, "I won't fight you."

* * *

The same morning that Eric had agreed to move out, a formal document from Donna Sheffield arrived at the house by special delivery. He studied it for a long time, turning it over once as if its mystery might be answered by something written on the back, and then he read it again. The enclosed document, she explained, was called *nolle prosequi*, which, in lay language, meant a decision not to prosecute, and she wrote: "*State of New Jersey vs. Nordblum* charges have been dropped as a case of mistaken identity." Her signature, as Radcliff, New Jersey's City Prosecutor was as miniscule as a whisper.

In a robot-like state, Eric left the house in the gray Pontiac and drove to David Rothberg's office in the city, parked at a fifteen-minute meter and rushed across the multistory atrium of the Zeckendorf Towers to the elevator. Storming through the lobby of the fifth floor to Rothberg's reception room, Eric slapped a check for the balance of Rothberg's fee on his secretary's desk.

Back in his car before the fifteen minutes had elapsed, Eric drove directly home. Shelly had asked if he could possibly leave before the boys came home from school, which was fine with him because the longer he stayed, the harder it would be to go. He loaded a suitcase and a few shirts on hangers into the car. High overhead, a hawk drifted, lazily dipped, and turned on widespread wings in a sky that looked like glass about to shatter, which was, he realized, precisely how he felt.

* * *

CHAPTER THIRTY-ONE

Mistaken identity?

Donna had said in her official documents that the case against Nordblum was being dropped due to mistaken identity.

That was it?

After all Tony had gone through to nail Nordblum, after the agony of jeopardizing everything, it hadn't occurred to him that the memo about the robbery in Arizona would not only have come to *his* attention, but also to the chief's and the prosecutor's. Whatever she wanted to call it, in his mind, the prosecutor really dropped the case due to lack of evidence. He had gambled on someone finding those goddamn 9 mm shells in the Pontiac, but no one had. Or maybe he just hadn't been told. If they had been found, they *couldn't* have been discounted as meaningless. And then that pathetic salesgirl in New Jersey recanted on her ID—which she had signed under oath. *But, shit, he had signed that goddamn affidavit under oath, too.* And of course, no gun was ever found.

"It was the affidavit," Dan was saying in a murderous tone, snapping Tony back to attention. He and Bernie were sitting opposite Dan and the office door was shut. "You gave Judge Barrington a load of crap which was not only beyond the realm of truth, it was a downright fabrication.

Filled with lies. You showed absolutely no consideration for Nordblum's rights." He was glaring directly at Bernie.

"I know, sir," Bernie said.

"But our intention was . . ." Tony began.

"Shut up," Dan told him. "I don't want to hear about your intentions. I'm talking about facts."

"I made a horrible mistake in judgment, Chief," Bernie said. His voice came through to Tony as if echoing down a metal tunnel.

"I guess the fuck you did," Dan said, still glaring directly at Bernie. "You put Radcliff on the map and then made us a laughingstock."

He pounded his fist on his desk, coffee splashing everywhere. He didn't seem to notice.

"Bernie and I . . ."

"I said to shut up, Tony. Bernie has confessed to lying to the judge."

"But . . ." Tony was speechless. What the hell was going on here? Bernie had refused to look at him even when Tony tapped his shoulder and leaned forward trying to see his face. He could usually tell what Bernie was thinking, but now he was looking at a blank wall.

"What do you mean confessed? We both . . ."

Dan jumped to his feet. "If you can't keep your mouth shut, then get the hell out of here, Tony. Here's what's coming down. Bernie, you are going on a two-week suspension starting now. Sit down. I'm not finished. And then, it's back to the academy with you."

"Yes, sir," Bernie responded compliantly. Tony was confused. All of Dan's accusations were directed at Bernie. And each time Tony tried to explain, Dan cut him off.

Bernie shouldn't be taking all the blame on this. They were partners, a team. Could Bernie be thinking he was paying Tony back for that time when he was accused of cheating in 9th grade? Tony had sworn to the teacher that Bernie had *not* been taking answers to the math test from his paper.

"What about me, Chief?" Tony asked.

"You both get written reprimands for signing an affidavit containing misleading information," Dan continued. "They'll be put in your records. Get your stuff together, Pigeon. Your two weeks are beginning right now. So, get out! And you . . ." he added as soon as they were alone, "you . . . you listen to me. Bernie is taking the fall for this. That's what Angelo wants and that's the end of it. No further discussion with anyone, especially Bernie. Do I make myself clear?"

"Yeah, Chief, but I sure don't get it . . ."

"You don't have to get it. Just consider this screwed-up investigation a closed issue." Tony heard the finality of Dan's voice followed by a silence that lasted so long that he thought Dan may have forgotten he was there. Tony was doing all he could to prevent a muscle in his leg from tightening.

Dan finally looked squarely at Tony. "You can turn in that uniform," he said in a voice as though the words were choking him. "As of today, you've made detective."

"Wow, Chief! What're you saying?"

"I'm saying you are Detective Deluca as of this moment. Now, get the hell out of here."

"Thanks, Chief, I won't screw this up. Never again." His cramping muscle relaxed. *Detective Deluca,* Tony whispered to himself; it rolled off his tongue like honey.

How many times in a person's life are they offered a second chance? Not to go back and change how they did things, but rather the opportunity to do things differently. The honorable way. The honest way. Jesus, he'd never again manufacture evidence or twist the truth. Never. And he felt badly about what had happened to Nordblum. In his half sleep, he'd written a million letters, conjuring up an apology for what he had done to the man. He'd actually gone to confession, looking for forgiveness. But that wasn't enough. He would pray for a second chance to somehow come to Eric Nordblum, too.

Even though the Chief was essentially forgiving him, he had noticed over the last few days that Dan's attitude toward him had changed. Now Tony sensed that, buried inside his words, there was a hard pellet of distrust or anger. He wasn't sure what, but he wasn't about to question it.

And believe me, I'm going to make it up to Bernie. As soon as I can. Whatever he wants.

Tony had just closed Dan's office door behind him when he was struck by a sudden realization. This was totally Pop's doing. Now all the recent shifts and realignments in Tony's life seemed crystallized in this new knowledge.

The scandal in Radcliff, like so much else in his life, moved to the periphery of Tony's awareness. Probably because he pushed it there.

* * *

"Hello, Tony, this is your Pop calling."

Tony figured that he was no doubt looking for an explanation or an apology. *Wait . . . had he just said "Pop"?*

"I want to congratulate you on making detective." His father's voice reached through the phone line like an embrace.

Not yet attuned to the nuanced change in Angelo's tone, Tony wanted to explain.

"I did everything by the book until it looked like my case was falling apart," he said. "Honest, I wouldn't have misled the judge or done other things if I hadn't been totally convinced that Nordblum was our man." It was those other things that brought shame to Tony's face. He could feel it spread across his cheeks like a fever, like a rash for all to see.

"I understand, son."

Still not listening, Tony's words tumbled one over the other. "Bernie shouldn't take the fall. It was both of us. But mainly, me. I kept remembering that you had said, 'Get the bastard, no matter what.'"

"Bernie confessed," his father assured him. "That's good enough for me."

"But . . ."

"You did the best you could with what you had. Any good cop would've done the same."

He's just saying that, Tony told himself, *but the fact that he* is *saying that means a lot.*

"You're gonna let Bernie back in, aren't you? He still wants to be a detective."

"Don't worry about Pigeon. We're taking care of him. He'll be back before you know it. Now, Detective Deluca, how about lunch today at Sherman's . . . just you and me?"

For a moment Tony was literally speechless. His father had forgiven him. And as for lunch . . . "Yes," he managed to say. "I'd like that. I'd really like that, His Honor."

"Okay son, see you at noon."

Had he said son? Had he referred to himself as Pop? Tony felt a cloud lifting and with it went his guilt about Bernie. He would think of many ways to thank his best buddy. The world was looking up for Tony. At least that was how it appeared. Of course, he reminded himself, he'd been wrong before. Whistling, he grabbed his keys and headed out, feeling more optimistic than he ever had.

* * *

CHAPTER THIRTY-TWO

"Why are you calling?" Eric asked when Maggie reached him at the Y in Albany four months later.

"Why?" he asked again, feeling anxious, yet even then it seemed an important question. Looking at his watch, he imagined her out for a power-walk with her honey-blonde hair maybe pulled back in a ponytail. Before, on days he had been in the office, they had often taken vigorous walks together during the lunch hour.

"Please don't ask me that," Maggie said and waited. He had the sensation that they were magnets, now only connected by the stream of his pain.

"The job in Pennsylvania didn't work out and this second one is just okay," he told her, listening to his words float through the phone and slowly break apart. The months since he had left home were a blur. Nights until closing, in any local bar. Late to work most mornings. *I would have fired me, too.*

"I'm just calling to see how you're doing."

"Better, I guess." Better was safe, a relative word. At least he wasn't hitting the booze as much, mainly because it had done a job on his gut. The pain had been excruciating. Which was worse? The pain in his stomach or the pain in his heart? Was it just the bitterness of rejection or the loss of all he had been?

"Better is good, Eric," Maggie said in what sounded to him like a slogan for a constipation product. Maybe that was appropriate—all his hatred of that pig-cop Deluca was trapped inside him, like crap stuck in his gut that was too hard and too rotten to expel.

"I guess so," was all he could manage.

"I'll check in with you again soon. Take care." And with that, Maggie hung up, breaking the tenuous connection to his former life.

* * *

A month later, Eric moved again, this time to Long Island for a position with yet another firm. Even he had to admit that things were improving. Now, he went to work early and stayed late. And he had an apartment where every night he ate a frozen dinner, watched an hour of news, took two Tylenol PMs, and went to bed. Even while he slept, held just beneath the surface of consciousness by the ballast of drugs, he knew there was something improbable in his dreams. Invariably, he would wake into darkness, confused and agitated.

Weekends, he watched more TV. No gardening for him, no puttering around the house, no raking leaves or shoveling snow to look forward to with the boys. His clarinet languished in the trunk of his car. No children, no wife. Just keep working his ass off and sending money to Shelly, the bottomless pit. And don't forget college— she didn't need to keep reminding him that *that* financial responsibility was looming. Never mind that the house *that he was paying for but didn't live in* was hocked up to the goddamn eyeballs. Thanks again Deluca, you fucker.

* * *

"Hi Artie, how's it going, son?"

"Okay, Dad."

"I've been following the Tigers' progress. You're undefeated. That's great."

"Yeah, it is. Hey, Dad, I gotta go, the guys are waiting."

"Wait, let me speak to Jason."

"He's not here. You wanna talk to Mom?"

Suddenly, Shelly was on the line. "Don't take it personally," she told him. "They're not avoiding you. It's just that they are busy with their own stuff. I hardly even see them myself."

Yeah. Sure.

Eric hardly recognized the confidence she exuded. It was clear to him that something was gone forever from their relationship.

These calls to the boys were becoming more and more awkward and full of silent stretches. Talking with Shelly was even worse. He was feeling more detached, clearly aware that his life meant nothing to them. It meant little to him as well.

"As long as I have you on the line Eric, I wanted to tell you that the boys and I are spending Thanksgiving, and Christmas too, with my family in Maine. I want them to get past the painful memories of last year's holidays."

"Both holidays?"

"I'd hoped you'd understand, Eric. We have to put the boys' feelings first."

What about his painful feelings? He knew what Thanksgiving was like with her family—two eighteen-pound turkeys, everybody's favorite desserts, going for a group walk in the crisp Maine air after eating yourself into oblivion, sitting around the fireplace, dozing within the embrace of a loving family . . .

"Yes, I guess I understand," he said. But it was an effort not to ask who would carve the turkeys.

* * *

Doctor Barthe, Eric's new shrink since he moved to Long Island, had agreed with Shelly. "Boys growing away from their parents is normal and would probably have happened even if you were not living far away."

"I doubt that," he had told her. "You don't know how close we were before my life hit the fan."

"Young teenagers, especially boys, rarely have time for their parents," she insisted. "They consciously lock you out of their lives. It's the first step toward manhood."

Manhood. What in Christ's name was that? Manhood is a myth that can be stolen away in the blink of an eye or by a rap on the door of a rented apartment on an ordinary afternoon.

He should always keep trying and eventually they would come around. At least that's what Dr. Barthe kept saying. But what the hell would she know? What could she possibly know about losing everything, about the hell he had descended into? He had nothing and it wasn't his fault.

Okay, the affair had been his fault, but they had gotten past that; things had been on the mend. He and Shelly would have been all right, if this hadn't happened.

He looked around his apartment, at the pathetic furnishings that had come with it; furniture that told stories of miserable transient people who, for one reason or another, had failed in their lives. He hated the stale smell of other peoples' habits. That's how he must smell—just like his apartment, like mold growing on him as he sat in the stagnant air of a one-window apartment; a window that had been nailed shut with him inside.

* * *

Out of the blue, Maggie called again in late October. "I see from your new number that you've moved again," she said accusingly. "Why didn't you let anyone know?"

Her voice slipped into his silence like early morning mist across a marsh. "Guess what?" she continued not waiting for a response. "I've been canned, too. Good old Mr. Johansen claimed they had to cut back and I came under the category of last in, first out. What do you think of that?"

Eric didn't know how to respond. Their situations were not in the least bit similar, yet he found himself wanting to show some kind of sympathy.

"That's lousy," he told her, certain that he should say something more but unable to find the words. He heard her take a deep breath.

"Anyway," she said, "I've been looking at three different job options, two right in New York City and one out near you on the Island. I think I'm ready for a complete change."

A long pause followed and he sensed that she had probably dared herself to say what she had just told him and was waiting for an encouraging response from him. The trouble was he didn't know how he felt. Certainly it was nothing he had expected to have to consider.

"Look, Maggie, I just want you to know that there's no going back. What we did was a mistake."

"I know that, Eric. You told me that before. But you're not with Shelly anymore, and *that's* not because of what *we* did. Can't we just be friends?"

Dr. Barthe would have told him not to be negative. Why did he keep going back to a shrink, anyway? Maybe some of her psychobabble shit was actually seeping into his subconscious.

"I'm not ready for anything like that."

"Just friendship?"

Eric couldn't think of what to say or quite how to say it.

"Well, why don't you take the one on the Island?" he answered finally. "I mean, you can if you want to." It was a lame response and he knew it. His throat suddenly felt dry.

"That would be wonderful!" she exclaimed. "I'll contact the company on Long Island first thing Monday morning and try to wrap things up here within the week."

He could tell by her voice that she was relieved that he had responded as he had.

"Thanks, Eric, I still think the world of you..." and then, as if afraid of what she might say next, she hung up, leaving him, in spite of what he had told her, to deal with a sudden rush of happiness, a feeling he hardly remembered.

* * *

CHAPTER THIRTY-THREE

The past year and a half had been nearly unbearable for Eric—an uncontested divorce with only brief visits with his sons, three different jobs, three different apartments, and weekly appointments with Dr. Barthe, his latest shrink. At the age of thirty-nine, Eric now realized that his sole relief from depression was through Maggie. She had moved to an apartment that he had located for her two blocks away from his. The big difference between them was that, for Maggie, it was a move she was clearly happy to make. In fact, Eric discovered she was positive about most things. And her apartment reflected that. It was a sunny, cheerful place that never failed to raise his spirits. And when the job that she moved to Long Island for hadn't panned out, she had immediately gone to a temp agency. There had been no depression or moping around for her. His shrink had told him that Maggie was good for him and that he was making excellent progress. *Maybe so.*

One evening, Maggie, whom he saw every few days now, invited him over for homemade lasagna and lemon meringue pie. Eric felt comfortable at her apartment which she had made cozy and welcoming with soft colors and a smell of cinnamon. Once Shelly had attempted lemon meringue pie and it had turned out flat. Maggie's meringue was at least three inches high. He told her it was delicious.

"It's my Aunt Marion's recipe. She lived in Mount Vernon, Maine and I always loved our annual August visit there. Her pantry was magical."

Maggie's smile was magical and he wondered, for the millionth time since she had moved to the Island, why she was standing by him. She made no emotional demands of him which turned their short-lived fling so long ago into fiction. How could she act so understanding? So . . . patient? They could never recapture the heat of their affair, he wouldn't want to and he doubted that she did either. It was her kindness that undid him. That and her cooking.

Over coffee, she commented to Eric about a news item that had caught her eye regarding a wrongful arrest lawsuit about a woman claiming her reputation had been damaged when the police had picked her up for shoplifting and then later realized she hadn't done it.

"I wonder if they took six months to figure that out for her, too." He couldn't stop himself. It was still sickening for Eric just to *think* Tony's name.

"Well, if that woman could sue for a damaged reputation, why couldn't you sue for a ruined life?" Maggie tilted her head to the side, an endearing habit that she had when she asked a question, her hair curling around her face, the color of honey.

"I think you should sue the butt off that bastard cop and the town of Radcliff, too. Get him for defamation of character, or whatever an attorney can dream up. You deserve to get some assurance that he's punished or thrown off the force," Maggie told him, warming to the idea. "Anything that will prevent him from ever being in the position to do that to someone again."

Her urgency seemed to push her to the edge of her chair; her freckles stood out prominently across her nose. "Don't you agree with me?"

"Maggie, Maggie, slow down." Eric stood and looked down at her. "I don't want anything to do with the police or lawyers or the friggin' justice system. I've hardly recovered my sanity. Thanks mainly to your support," he added softly, looking around the little living room, pushing down an impulse to flee.

"But, Eric . . ."

"Listen to me. It would mean I'd have to relive the whole nightmare. It would tear open a wound that is barely healed. I'm sorry but I can't do it." Neither of them spoke for a few minutes. Moonlight slanted through the window and cast shadows on the painted floor.

Maggie changed the subject. But the seed of an idea had been planted.

*　*　*

"Maggie," Eric called as he stepped into her apartment a few days later, her lily-of-the-valley scent greeting him. "I'm going to do it! I'm going to call Frank Delmar, my first lawyer in New Jersey, and ask him to come back on board. I'm going to sue Deluca and the whole damn town of Radcliff." He wanted her to look at him. He needed to see if she shared his excitement. It was the most defining moment of his new life.

Her eyes brimmed with tears as she opened her arms to him, but when she kissed him, he went still, like a captive animal that doesn't *not* resist, yet remains slightly stiff, vigilant. He felt his body sing. He closed his eyes, terrified to wrap his arms around her, even more terrified that she might pull away. He hadn't been wanted like this for so long; love hadn't been declared to him as guilelessly, without reserve. His heart slammed against the inside of his ribs.

They were past talking. He put his hands on either side of her face, his eyes intense and yearning and he kissed her—long and sensual. Pushing her back, he felt her melt to the floor. She pulled him close and brushed her lips over his chest. Nothing was rushed; he felt no sense of urgency.

"Darling," he breathed into her ear, finally letting himself go.

Afterward, they lay entangled, their bodies pulsed with aftershocks, and she slid her arms around him, holding him close so that his grateful face was buried against the curve of her neck, and his breath fell between the buttons of her blouse.

"Shall I stay tonight?" he said, and felt her smile against his skin.

* * *

Eric told Dr. Barthe that, after all this time, he felt emotionally stable enough to seek restitution for his wrongful arrest. However, she had said that as long as he was only thinking of revenge, he wasn't ready.

Although he understood what she was driving at, in his opinion, revenge should simply be classified as justice. Of course, the revenge Eric had been dreaming of for so long was aimed directly at Tony Deluca, the despicable liar, the man who, at untold cost to Eric, for some malicious sick reason, had acted without conscience. The bottom line was that, whatever you wanted to call it, whatever Deluca's motivations had been, he had wantonly destroyed Eric's life as he had known it.

But until now, Eric had had no place to go with his anger.

✽ ✽ ✽

With this burst of positive energy and direction, Eric had no problem calling Frank Delmar, who agreed to meet with him at his office in Trenton. While Maggie waited in the lobby, Eric took the elevater up to the fourth floor and found himself thinking about Arthur and Jason. He needed to do this if for nothing more than to prove to his boys that he had been innocent. His driving need to retrieve their respect was rekindled; to show them the terrible injustice of what had happened. And maybe, deeper in his subconscious than he was prepared to look, there lurked a hidden desire to point out how their mother had left him, kicked him when he was down.

"I want justice for the humiliation of having been arrested and *put in jail,*" Eric said, the minute he was seated across the desk from Frank. Behind him was a walnut file cabinet, replete, no doubt, with half a century of pledges, breaches, and secrets, probably even including the details of his unjust arrest. "And that's not all. I want to recoup at least some of the fortune I spent in legal fees."

"We can do more than that, Eric," the attorney told him. "We can certainly bring a civil suit against the City of Radcliff, and particularly, Anthony Deluca, but you can also include the Chief of Police and, of course, Deluca's sidekick, Bernie Pigeon. Possibly the prosecutor, too, but let me think about that."

"The standard for most liability claims against law enforcement agencies is the concept of reckless indifference, which a plaintiff alleges if a person, acting under the cover of law, lies about pertinent information that is relevant to their course of action," Frank explained.

Eric sat rigid, listening closely. "Those bastards not only ignored what I said, but they lied through their teeth about it."

"The terrible injustice of what they have done to you, Eric, can and should be exposed and punished legally through a civil case," Frank assured him. "They're *all* liable."

"What about my personal losses? The intangible ones?"

"Absolutely. You're entitled to a claim for that, too."

"All right then, let's proceed," Eric said, pushing Dr. Barthe's words about revenge deep in the back of his mind. "What I want is for Anthony Deluca to never work as a police officer again. In fact, what I would *really* like is for him to spend time in jail, to go through the entire degrading admitting process, just like I had to."

"He sure as hell deserves it," Frank concurred.

A weight seemed to lift from Eric's shoulders. The process had begun.

When Eric and Maggie left Frank's building, they walked briskly to the old Pontiac, hardly aware that they were holding hands.

✼ ✼ ✼

The next week, when Frank called for another meeting, Eric went alone. He had noticed that the flood of optimism he felt after the first meeting had been followed by moments of apprehension that the entire rotten crew from Radcliff might come after him again if Frank exposed them.

When he had told Dr. Barthe, she had assured him that these were healthy signs of dealing with buried emotions. *That was easy for her to say. He was the one who thinks he is having a heart attack every time a blue light and a shrieking siren gains speed behind him on the highway.*

After Frank thoroughly outlined the case as he planned to present it, he filled Eric in on the timetable. "Depositions will have to be taken and a trial date set. It'll probably be six months before we get in front of a judge."

"That's okay with me. I've waited so long that another few months means nothing. And look, Frank, I have what might be a strange request. I only want to be in the courtroom when you have Deluca on the stand. Other than that, I know I couldn't bear to sit through the jury selection or any bullshit arguments and pathetic excuses put forth by the defendants."

Eric believed that the healing process he had been working on with his therapist, and now with Maggie, would be seriously compromised by his even being in the same space with those people who would be attempting to justify their crime against him.

It *had* been a crime, and he, for one, was not going to forget about it.

* * *

CHAPTER THIRTY-FOUR

Five months later, the call he had been waiting for came. Eric's breath froze when Frank told him it was time to come.

"Deluca will be on the stand the day after tomorrow," he said. "The Trenton courthouse at nine in the morning. Are you up for it?" Eric knew that there had been a change of venue to Trenton, since any jury in Radcliff would have been so prejudicial that they would not have been able to seat an unbiased jury. He was encouraged to hear something close to excitement in Frank's voice.

The minute Eric stepped into the municipal building, he felt nauseous. A wave of apprehension and loneliness swept over him. Maggie had offered to come along, but he had decided this final personal journey needed to be traveled alone.

Eric was surprised that so many people had been galvanized by his case. He could understand residents from Radcliff being there since it must appear to them that the entire foundation of their city was under siege, but other people in attendance were there out of curiosity or perhaps wondering if the public servants in their communities were corrupt as well.

The din in the courtroom turned to a hush when the chamber door opened abruptly and the bailiff stepped out. "All rise," he called out in a resonating voice.

Judge Geoffrey B. Farnsworth, draped in his black robe, emerged from chambers and moved ponderously to his chair on the dais overlooking the courtroom.

Deliberately keeping his eyes averted from the jury box and especially from the other side of the aisle where the defendants sat, Eric was relieved to just focus on the judge.

His heart was pounding when Delmar called Mr. Anthony Angelo Deluca's name.

* * *

Tony walked to the stand with what could pass for a surprisingly jaunty step. His lawyer had told him to show confidence, but actually he was nervous and even a little scared. The last year and a half had been idyllic, everything he had ever wanted his life to be; his relationship with Pop had blossomed, and he was a regular at Pop's Friday night dinners at Shirley's. And of course once Bernie had finished his classes, they had teamed up as detective partners. All this had been *before* this Nordblum nightmare resurfaced a few months ago. Ever since then, everyone seemed to be avoiding him. Tony supposed it was because they were going over strategies about how to handle the case. He had certainly spent a lot of time with his lawyer.

Eric was shocked when he saw Tony for the first time in almost two years. He appeared so much smaller than he had remembered; rather insignificant, actually.

The clerk swore him in and as soon as he was seated, Frank began his questioning.

"Please give your name and address."

"Anthony Angelo Deluca, 444 Chester Street, Radcliff, New Jersey."

Tony searched the courtroom until he located his father, hoping for a reassuring nod, but Pop was stone-faced. He had been aloof ever since he and Dan started to huddle together with the town counselor about two months ago.

"In your deposition, you said you were concerned about retaliation by Mr. Nordblum," the lawyer was saying. "Have you received any threats by or through Eric Nordblum? Or through his counsel in this case?"

"No, I have not," Tony replied.

"What was it about your conduct in connection with this case that made you feel Mr. Nordblum might wish to retaliate?"

"I didn't have any *conduct* in this case," Tony said defensively. "I don't know any reason he would have to retaliate. But I still felt cautious."

"Do you perhaps have a guilty conscience?"

"No. For what?" Tony shrugged heavily as though shifting a weight from one shoulder to another.

"Are you a high school graduate?"

"Yes, sir, I am."

"What kind of training have you had in order to become a police officer?"

"Police Academy. Then there's an interview."

"Did you complete your police training?"

"Yes, sir." He must know the answers to these questions, Tony thought. Why didn't he just get on with it?

"Is the reason you were hired as a police officer for the city of Radcliff because your father was the mayor and the police chief was his friend?"

"No," Tony said, genuinely outraged. "I was hired on my own merit."

"Is there any specific training that's required within the Radcliff Police Department to be promoted from patrol officer to detective?"

"Mainly, good performance and evaluations," Tony said, shrugging. "And a recommendation from a staff officer."

"When you became involved in this case, you had been a police officer for about four years. Is that correct?"

"That's right." Tony did not like this lawyer; there was a mean look in his eyes.

"Now," he said, "I would like to discuss the different levels of disciplinary action that are incorporated when necessary in the Radcliff Police Department. Would I be correct in observing that there are four levels; oral reprimands, written reprimands, suspension, and termination in that ascending order of severity?"

"I don't know what you mean by that question," Tony said, frowning.

"Are you telling this jury that you can't tell them whether a reprimand is more or less severe than termination?"

"I could answer that question, but it depends on; you know . . . who did what to whom."

Eric was stunned. So he was stupid, too. That bastard couldn't even answer a logical question. When Eric thought of how he had hammered him with his outrageous interrogation. Question after question, and to think that he'd assumed the guy knew what he was doing.

"On November 29th, almost two years ago, you were dispatched to Gordon's International Department Store in Radcliff by Chief Daniel Fortini," Frank said. "Is that correct?"

"Yes, I was sent there."

"At that time, did the chief give you details about a diamond-stealing scam going on at other Gordon's stores in the Northeast?"

"Yes sir, he did." No one could say he wasn't being cooperative.

"Now, you and Chief Fortini decided, did you not, that this would be a good place to set-up a stakeout or a sting operation. Is that correct?"

"Yes sir," he said, "I was to confront them once they were on the sidewalk."

"And your chief told you to wait outside the store, across the street. The plan was that the criminals were going to be allowed to pull off the scam and walk out with the diamond. By that time, you would have been alerted by the manager and would arrest them with the goods, so to speak, after they exited. Is that correct?"

"Yes," he said, "I was to confront them once they were out on the sidewalk."

"However, you, Mr. Deluca, you were not alert or ready to confront these robbers as planned, and as a result, there was a shooting, right?"

"That's not true," Tony protested angrily, "I *was* ready. But, Mr. Richardson got in the way. I had told him to stay inside and let me handle the situation, but he ran out and messed everything up. They could have shot me, as well."

Tony gave a quick glance over at Dan who was glaring at him. Acid rose up from his gut and hit the back of his throat. He swallowed hard and reached for the glass of water sitting on the railing.

"Excuse me, Mr. Deluca," the lawyer said, "but I must ask you to just answer my questions. Your conduct in connection with this matter was noted in your police file, was it not?"

"What conduct? Tony exclaimed. "I haven't seen that file; I don't know what it said."

"An investigative report of the incident was filed, which stated that you were *not* ready, and did *not* respond promptly to Mr. Richardson's call."

Tony's thoughts congealed in confusion. His report had never said anything like that. He sat there stunned and momentarily speechless.

"Did you receive any disciplinary action other than the written report that was put in your personal record?"

"No, sir."

"In your deposition, you claimed that you were concerned but not embarrassed by the written reprimand in your official police record. Is that correct?"

"Yes."

"And what was the measure of your concern? How would you characterize the scope and depth of your concern?"

"Only that it could go against me if I were ever to move to another precinct."

"Did the fact that your father was mayor of Radcliff have any effect on your performance or the evaluation of you as a police officer?"

Well, it was clear where this man was going now. And Tony didn't want to go there. His "no" rang loud and clear in the courtroom.

"Did he squash this reprimand for you?"

"No, sir. Definitely not."

"Do you know what the policy of the Radcliff Police Department is for disciplinary action for an officer who instructed a citizen to turn over an $8,000 item to known thieves, and who allowed a citizen to expose himself to personal harm because the officer wasn't at the ready? Tell me, sir, what action is meted out for that?"

"I don't believe I could answer that."

Tony felt a sense of panic building within him at all that he didn't know about the reports; at all he *did* know and couldn't change. And anger too. Yes, he felt anger that came in a sudden rush.

"Don't you think that's appropriate for termination?"

"No, sir, I don't."

"Is it appropriate for suspension?"

"That decision would be on a case-by-case basis."

"With only a written reprimand, you were then elevated to detective status and given the job of solving this crime. Is that correct?"

"No, sir," Tony admitted, "I was never anything but a patrolman until later."

"The Radcliff Police Department had a unique opportunity, in that it was aware ahead of the fact that a crime was about to take place. You had these people in your grasp and they shot a citizen and slipped away with an expensive diamond belonging to a taxpayer of the city of Radcliff. Is that true?"

"If you consider the store a taxpayer, yes. But the way I see it, a taxpayer is a regular person, not like a business."

"Were you embarrassed by what occurred?"

"Embarrassed? No, why should I be?"

Tony's saliva turned to sawdust.

"Certainly if you weren't embarrassed, you wouldn't have had any occasion to lie about how it happened to anybody else, would you?"

"I wasn't embarrassed and I didn't lie to anyone," Tony told him, deciding he should stop looking at his father for encouragement.

"How about to Detective Fornier in Kensington when you told him you were on surveillance waiting across the street for the suspects and the manager did not alert you? You weren't lying then?"

"No. I was there and ready."

Tony looked at Bernie to see how he was taking all this. A lot depended on his going along with Tony's story. Their eyes locked for an instant and then Bernie looked away, took off his glasses, and rubbed his eyes with both fists.

"I represent to you that Detective Fornier testified in his deposition that you did tell him that. Is he lying?"

"I wouldn't say he's lying exactly. If I did speak to him, which I don't remember, he may have not understood fully what I was saying . . ."

Tony's voice faltered and faded into a whisper. He had never felt more alone in his life.

"I see. Or does it not, sir, perhaps reflect your intense embarrassment about what really happened?"

"The reason I wasn't embarrassed was if the Gordon's manager would have done what he was supposed to have done, I probably would have caught those people."

"Precisely what are you telling me that the manager failed to do?"

"Mr. Richardson was supposed to notify me when those people came into the store."

"Are you saying he did not?"

"That's right, sir."

Tony was reminded of a childhood refrain; *liar, liar, pants on fire*.

"Then why was a reprimand entered in your personal file?"

"The reprimand was not for that."

"Did I read it wrong?" the lawyer asked him. "It says here, and let me quote: 'Mr. Deluca was not alert and ready to confront these robbers.' I see nothing that says that the store failed to call as planned. Here, let me show it to you."

"It must be a mistake. Let me see."

Tony took the file from Frank and started to read it. *Oh no! They'd changed the report. Somebody is selling me out. What the hell is going on? Jesus, help me!*

"It doesn't say anything about the store failing to call, does it?"

"It was supposed to."

Eric leaned forward, waiting, listening intently for every nuance, for any hint that Tony felt the slightest remorse for what he had done. From the look on his face, Eric couldn't be sure if Tony was anything but confused at this point.

"Okay," Frank said pleasantly, "we'll get back to that later. Now, Mr. Deluca, based on the descriptions in the original composite, which of these two males in the photographs I am showing you did you believe was Mr. Nordblum? The one with the mustache?"

"No. The one without the mustache is Nordblum."

"How did you come to that conclusion?"

"One precinct reported a suspect with a mustache and another one without."

"So you never had one witness who told you that he or she had seen the same man, once with a mustache and once without it, did you?"

"No, I did not," Tony said defiantly.

"In fact, after this incident occurred," the lawyer persisted, "you never asked Mr. Richardson for an oral narrative description of anyone, did you?"

"Are you talking about after the shooting occurred? I don't understand . . . I don't know if I did or I didn't. If he had given me one, I would have put it in my report."

This bastard lawyer was talking in circles and he was doing it on purpose to trip him up. Where the hell had all this information come from, anyway?

"And if he didn't give you a description, it was because you never asked him, isn't that so?"

'Well, I don't know if I asked him or not," Tony muttered. "Maybe he wasn't able to give me one. I don't know."

"Wouldn't you have made a note of that in your report?"

If this bastard is expecting a yes or no on this one, he was going to be disappointed.

"I could have, yes. Or then again, I might not have."

"Can we agree to one thing, that *not* to have asked him for a description was a major omission and poor police procedure?"

"Not necessarily," Tony replied, aware that he was being pushed into a corner. "I had a positive ID from the salesgirl who was robbed in Mr. Richardson's store, and one from her manager. That was enough for me."

Tony felt his back stiffen and his lungs expand beyond endurance.

"I see," the lawyer said, thoughtfully. "Of course the reason you didn't ask Mr. Richardson for a description and the reason you didn't ask him to participate in the creation of the composite and the reason you never went back to him and showed him your photo lineup was because you didn't want to face him, isn't that so?"

"No, that's not true at all," Tony argued. "I'm not saying there weren't some mistakes in my report, but to say I was embarrassed to go see Mr. Richardson, I don't think that's accurate."

Tony stole a glance at Eric who looked as though he was enjoying watching him squirm. He could only imagine how much the man must hate him.

"Now, going back to when you and Officer Pigeon went to Connecticut to check the lead that had come in about one Ivan Petroff, a man that nobody else had pursued for further investigation, you concluded as well that he did not match the composites or the narrative description. Is that right?"

"That's correct. I didn't believe that he took the diamond. But he ID'd Mr. Nordblum and when I saw Mr.

Nordblum's gray Pontiac, the car that matched the one at the robbery, that was enough for me. Don't forget, I was there."

Tony took a deep breath. Maybe he'd pay attention to that fact.

"So, you claim that the connection between Mr. Nordblum and these crimes was his car, is that right?"

"Yes, and after I got through interviewing him, I was sure he was the one."

"His car, huh? Well, let's see. You knew four things about the getaway car: It was full-sized, it was dark gray in color, and it had a bent antenna. And you wrote down the license number. Is that correct?"

"Yeah, but that didn't pan out. We couldn't find a match."

"And when Mr. Nordblum told you that he bent his antenna in a carwash, did you check that out?"

"No. I mean, yes. I spoke to the guy at the carwash, but he denied that it happened there."

Eric had heard about enough by the time the court took a morning break. Tony was actually pathetic, he thought. Even in court, even under oath, he couldn't stop lying to save his skin. Maybe this was the cathartic that Dr. Barthe had been talking about this past year. Perhaps this was how Eric was going to finally set himself free.

* * *

Out in the hall, Frank told Eric that his case had an unusual aspect to it, at least in his experience. He had never before been involved in a case where the jury, if they found in his client's favor, were entitled to award him not merely compensatory damages which would include what Eric spent out of his pocket, but punitive or exemplary damages against the defendants or such of them that they felt deserved to be punished.

"You're good, Frank," Eric told him. "Deluca is flip-flopping all over the place. I'm wondering when you're going to ask him about my DayTimer, why he never wanted to check my alibi. I can't wait to hear how he wiggles out of that one."

"I'm not going to. We don't need the DayTimer now because this entire case is based on the fact that Deluca demonstrated reckless indifference to your rights by lying to the judge on his affidavit. That's all I need to prove and we're halfway there."

Eric scrutinized Frank's face. He hoped to God he knew what he was doing. "It's incomprehensible to me how Deluca ever became a police officer, no less a detective."

"The way he's caving in," Frank agreed, "I'm thinking this is going to be a slam dunk. I can't predict how much you'll get, but the jury seems to be with us."

"I haven't looked at the jury," Eric told him. "I can barely look at Deluca on the stand. I'm just listening and picturing him questioning me back in my Dalton apartment."

Frank gave Eric a hard look. "You've got to let go of that. This trial provides the key for you to open that door and let all those poisonous memories out. Let them be gone forever, my friend."

When Tony came shuffling out of the men's room, his chin nearly resting on his chest, Eric hurried to the water fountain and remained there until he was sure that

Tony was out of sight. Whatever else happened, he had no intentions of any face-to-face interaction whatsoever with the man who, without giving it a second thought, had changed the course of his life forever.

* * *

After everyone was seated and Tony was back in the witness stand, the judge reminded him that he was still under oath.

"Now, Mr. Deluca," Frank began, "I would like to discuss the color of the getaway car. It was gray, wasn't it?"

"Yes, it was gray."

"And Mr. Nordblum's car is a two-tone gray, isn't it?" Frank inquired.

"Gray is gray in my mind," Tony replied sullenly. In his experience, lawyers always split hairs.

"Detective Popoulas of Sutton, Connecticut stated in his deposition that you told him the getaway car was exactly the same as Mr. Nordblum's car. Did you, or was he lying?"

"It was the same. It was gray and had a bent antenna."

"I see. So now we have another police officer from another jurisdiction who was mistaken."

"He must have been wrong," Tony said. "I'm not saying he lied, just that he was wrong. There was also a map of the area in Mr. Nordblum's car, which made me suspicious."

"Surely it's not grounds for suspicion to find a map in a car, is it?"

"I don't know. I just thought it was suspicious."

Tony, his mouth half open, lost track of what he was trying to say and stopped.

"Isn't that the problem with this entire investigation, Mr. Deluca? When your suspect didn't match descriptions and other evidence didn't fit the case, you would go back and change the descriptions or facts. Isn't that the problem with this entire case?"

"There's no problem with this case."

Tony's heart was beating erratically. Someone had changed the files. *It wouldn't be Pop. Not since we've become so close. It wasn't him. It couldn't be. And it positively wasn't Bernie. He would never betray me. Never. So, it had to be Dan. But, why?*

"Isn't the reason you pursued investigating Mr. Nordblum, even though you realized how absurd it had been to show Mr. Petroff the composites and to follow up on his lead, was because you had failed in your mission?" Frank persisted. "You were not alert and ready? Isn't that a fact?"

Eric began now to comprehend the enormous stupidity that had launched this entire travesty. This guy was unbelievable—God, the dark excruciating corners that people back themselves into. He doubted if Deluca would ever recover from his lies.

"I *was* alert and ready," Tony insisted. "Richardson got in the way, I told you that."

Tony was doing what his lawyer had told him. Stick to your story, *no matter what.* That's what he'd said.

"Is it a coincidence that one of the items missing from the Radcliff Police records when they were turned over to this counsel for the Plaintiff, was the picture of Mr. Nordblum's vehicle?"

Tony shot a quick look at Dan who looked deathly pale. *He looks guilty.*

"I know nothing about that," he muttered.

"Would you agree with me, Mr. Deluca, that an investigation is supposed to be a reasoned and logical process?"

"Most of the time, yes."

"Most of the time? All right. Would one of the reasons you didn't go back to Mr. Richardson with a picture of the vehicle be the same reason that you didn't involve him in the creation of your composite picture, the same reason you never showed him your photo line-up, which was that you were embarrassed to face him?"

"No, that's not true at all."

"When you had the composite made up, why in the world didn't you ask Mr. Richardson to look at it? Wasn't he the one who had the best opportunity to describe the thieves and to participate in that process?"

"I don't remember if I asked him or not."

"Would you agree that you should have?"

"I couldn't answer that right now," Tony hedged, "because I don't remember any conversations we had. I don't know whether he could identify them or not. If he was asked, he may have declined."

Tony told himself not to look at Richardson. His hands were so slick with sweat that he had to wipe them on his pants.

"Now, about the affidavit, Mr. Deluca. Because the crime had already been committed and you didn't have Mr. Nordblum in Radcliff, New Jersey, you had to get a warrant to proceed against him, right?"

"That's right."

"Proper identification is the best tool to prevent wrongful arrests," the lawyer told him. "But knowing the law is the second most important thing. The law requires that a decision be made by a judge as part of our great system of checks and balances. And only a court or a justice could issue such a warrant, right?"

"I think that's right."

"Your affidavit says that your original witnesses believed that Mr. Nordblum was the one who came into the store that day. Did you consider "believe" a sufficient identification to constitute probable cause and go for a warrant?"

"Sort of, but not in and of itself."

Tony's lawyer had told him not to stick his neck out in his answers. *That was another warning; don't say anything that they can use against you.*

"That's interesting, sir. Now, you said in your deposition that your interpretation was not that Mr. Nordblum probably did commit the crime, but that he *could have* committed it, is that correct?"

"I don't think I said it that way."

Eric knew by now that his decision to stay away from the trial had been a good one. To have sat through this kind of witness-questioning for days might have pushed him into assaulting one of them or at the very least, screaming in protest.

"I see. And when your witnesses looked at Mr. Nordblum's photograph, and said he looked the most like the suspect of the various ones you have here, do you call that a tentative ID?"

"Yes."

"And when you have a witness who is unwilling to go the extra mile to say, 'That's the man,' you call that a tentative ID?"

"That's correct. But for me, it's close enough."

"Are you aware of an obligation to tell nothing but the truth in preparing an affidavit and not to overstate the character of your evidence to the judge?"

"Yes."

Tony wished that Bernie had stopped him. Oh, how he wished he had. Or Chief? Or why hadn't he stopped himself from lying on that damn affidavit?

"If the person is not a real danger to the public," the lawyer continued, "judges think that it's not worth the liability of having a false arrest. Given that, were you aware of your obligation that if there were any major holes in your information to bring those to the judge's attention?"

"Could you clarify that?"

"Would you agree with me that it would not be proper procedure in seeking a warrant by deliberately using imprecise language to get past a thin spot in the evidence in order to get it by the judge?"

"I presented the evidence I had at the time. I believed in it. Don't forget, I was there."

Eric had all he could do to keep from leaping out of his chair in protest. Frank gave him a significant look. It was a kind of "got him" look.

"What would you have done, hypothetically, if Mr. Nordblum, on the occasion of your initial interview, had refused to answer any of your questions and instructed you to leave?"

"We would have left. But if we weren't able to get any cooperation from him, we would have had to get pictures somehow of his car and of him."

Eric froze when he heard this answer. Maybe he was equally as stupid as they were. Why had he let Deluca and Pigeon interrogate him in the first place, let alone take his picture? The fact that he had submitted to that interview would, he knew, always remain a mystery to him. He would probably take that question to his grave.

"This photograph you wanted to get—perhaps it would be taken surreptitiously?"

"I would have taken a picture of him when he came out into the street."

"In your meeting with Detective Fornier of Kensington, New York, did you tell him that you interviewed Mr. Nordblum?"

"No, I did not."

"So if he said that you did, that would be false. Is that correct?"

"That's correct."

Eric began listening with a curious detachment, as if this entire episode he was observing was something that he had stumbled on by accident, something that had nothing to do with him.

"Can you think of anyone else, other than you, that Detective Fornier might have obtained this information from at that point?"

Tony truly didn't remember this fabrication. Most of the lies he did remember, but not this one.

"I have no idea. I don't know. You're getting me confused. Could you repeat that?"

"How did he come up with that observation if it wasn't from you?"

"I didn't say he didn't get it from me. It's not uncommon for a police officer to question things like that. It may have been just a note I wrote down in my report. It could mean something at a later date."

"Do you have to explain what is and is not in your report?"

"Well, if it's not in the report, I can try to clarify . . ."

"It was an observation that you had made on your own and you repeated to Detective Fornier, isn't that right?"

"I guess so."

"So, a good police detective puts facts in his report and if he's indulging in speculation, he will indicate that it's speculation, am I correct?"

"Sometimes he does and sometimes he doesn't."

"Let me ask you this. Do you think that any good detective would state something as a fact that was actually pure speculation?"

"If, at the time, it was speculation, it could become a fact that I found out later. So it should just be put in the report as speculation."

"I'll try that one again, Mr. Deluca. My question to you is whether or not you're telling the jury that a good police detective would record as fact, something which was only speculation?"

"No. Well, maybe not. It depends."

Tony coughed, tears stood in his eyes. All he wanted to do was leap from the witness box and run to his father. He would beg for forgiveness. On his knees.

"When you told Detective Fornier as well as Detective Popoulas that Mr. Nordblum was into drugs and wearing a false mustache at the time of the theft, that was speculation, right?"

"Wait, I don't recall telling them that."

"Well, I put it to you, Mr. Deluca, that to this day you would still be denying the things that you said to Detective Fornier if you didn't know we had Detective Popoulas' deposition saying that the same things had been said to him, isn't that so?"

"That's not true. That's not what I said. I couldn't have."

"All right, Mr. Deluca, let's move on. The lineup photograph you assembled with Mr. Nordblum's face dead center. I suppose you're going to tell me that you don't know that it too is missing from the Radcliff police records."

"I don't know if it's missing. I had nothing to do with that."

Tony had to make a conscious effort to breathe. The air in the courtroom seemed thin, insubstantial. *Something sinister had taken place and he knew nothing about it.*

"The photo display was shown to Mary Fletcher, the salesgirl at the Gordon's store in Parkdale, New Jersey. She made a positive ID and her manager concurred. Is that correct?"

"Yes. They both made positive IDs."

"This was after Miss Fletcher had originally stated that she wasn't sure. Is that right, Mr. Deluca?"

"I don't know her exact words. But it's up to the people involved. If they both think alike and both do the same things, the chances are that they might be good witnesses, but then again, maybe not; it depends."

"I'll leave the interpretation of that to the jury," Frank said, and now Tony saw, he was smiling. "One last thing. Do you know anything about 9 mm bullets that were placed in Mr. Nordblum's Pontiac *after* it was impounded and searched?"

"*What?*"

Understanding came too late as horror spread over Tony's face.

"And did you in fact, Mr. Deluca, threaten Miss Fletcher in order to have her change her testimony? And finally, did you or did you not, Mr. Deluca, deliberately lie on that affidavit?"

Tony was struck with a whiplash of disbelief. *Bernie must have told. He must have told everything. They all must have collaborated—schemed behind his back. He was the sacrificial lamb.* He knew in his heart there would be no forgiveness, no going back. He was caught in an avalanche of paralyzing humiliation.

"Mr. Deluca, I'm waiting for an answer."

"Yes."

"Yes what, Mr. Deluca?"

"All of it."

With inhuman effort, Tony sent the tendrils of his mind out of the courtroom, away from his words, over the city and its houses and streets, back to Pleasant Pond where he and Bernie went fishing when they were both thirteen, young, and still innocent.

"All of what, Mr. Deluca?"

"I wasn't alert and ready."

"And?"

Tony, drained and broken, had nothing to hold on to but a single thread of truth.

"I lied," Tony said. "I admit it. I lied."

At last! He had said it! Eric felt a rush of conflicting emotions. But the anger? Where, he thought, had all the anger gone?

* * *

CHAPTER THIRTY-FIVE

Police Chief Daniel Fortini hurried to his car, avoiding eye contact with anyone. As soon as he was on his way back to Radcliff, he put on his flashers and made the trip in less than an hour. After stopping at the station to leave a note for Tony, he then drove straight to his house on Hawthorne Street, the house he had lived in his entire life.

Putting on his old Rutgers football jersey and shorts, Dan took off from the front porch, running two miles due east, then three. In the cool of a late November afternoon, sweat poured into his eyes and he gasped great drafts of air. Crows bickered in the field, and above, there was not a single cloud, yet, there was thunder somewhere. Passing the town line, he kept running until he realized that no matter how hard he tried, he could not outrace his fear or bitterness. Collapsing at the edge of the road, Chief Fortini buried his face in his hands, and sobbed.

* * *

The minute he was excused from the stand and Judge Farnsworth had left the courtroom for the lunch recess, Tony turned to search for his father in the back row and saw his face frozen in an expression of disapproval and disgust, an expression he had hoped never to see again.

"Pop!" Tony called out, and then, as Angelo Deluca moved heavily but steadily away him, "His Honor!"

By the time he had reached the parking lot, his father was gone. Leaning against his cruiser, Tony looked up at the grand brick building of the Trenton courthouse with its cascading steps and ionic columns before dropping into the driver's seat. Waves of darkness crashed over him.

As he traveled through downtown Trenton, he remembered, back in Radcliff years ago, going into Stevens' drugstore after school and sitting with Bernie and a bunch of kids at the fountain. And he remembered the scoops of chocolate ice cream in a tall glass frosted with ice, the whirr of the blender. The laughter among friends.

Funny, but the thought of ice cream made him feel ill.

He passed the dense traffic near the airport and emerged among the rolling hills of northern Jersey, driving so slowly now that the one and a half hour trip back took an extra hour. His mind was empty, his thoughts free-floating. One thing of which he was absolutely sure and that was that he dreaded returning to Radcliff.

Tony knew something had changed as soon as he walked into the station. First of all, no one looked at him. Then there was the note on his desk saying that the chief had stopped by and wanted to talk to him as soon as he got back from Trenton and that he should stay at the station and wait for him no matter what time it turned out to be. Tony's mind started racing in circles. His world existed in separate parts. His mother. His father. The Chief. Nordblum. Himself. *The lies. The jury couldn't have made up their minds already. Could they? Holy Mother of God, pray for me.* But he knew that the verdict wasn't what Dan wanted to talk to him about; it would be *Dan's* verdict. That's why the chief wanted to see him. *Tony knew.*

Struggling into his jacket, he rushed out the door. When he bounced his squad car onto the road, the rear wheels kicked up a spray of gravel that hung for several seconds in the air behind him.

His first stop would be *Everspring Cemetery*. He leaned forward over the wheel with an intense urgency, overcome with a longing so precise and painful that he felt his heart being squeezed, hot in his chest.

Ten minutes later, he stood in the cemetery in front of his mother's grave, marked by a pink granite monument, grand enough for the wife of a president, let alone the mayor of a small town in New Jersey. Stretching out full-length next to the mound topped with the bunch of wilted pink carnations that he had left a few days ago, Tony let the silence sink into him like a drug. If only he had looked at Nordblum's stupid DayTimer and seen his alibi, none of this would have happened. But then, he wouldn't have earned his way into his father's good graces—and finally made Pop proud.

But Tony realized with sudden clarity that he had been born with a brooding drive to succeed *no matter what*, the same trait he most feared in his father. It had, he thought, shuddering, been passed down to him like poison in the blood.

Oh, the sight of His Honor's broad back deliberately turned against him as he left the courtroom—not a glance of forgiveness, not an ounce of anything to hope for.

Startled awake by the honking of a flock of geese passing overhead, trailing their long ragged V-shape across the sky,

Tony, stiff and chilled to the bone, looked at his watch and saw that he had been asleep almost an hour. Getting to his feet, the November sun so low now it nearly blinded him, he took slow backward steps to the cruiser.

* * *

Tony drove slowly toward town on Route 4. As he approached the Deluca Bridge, he pulled over to the side of the road. Getting out of the cruiser, he leaned over the railing's edge and looked down at the river, dark and quiet below, where a skein of fog unraveled across the water. He swallowed against the lump in his throat that was studded with regret.

Without giving himself more time to think, Tony got back in the cruiser and drove for about a mile before taking a U-turn. He sat idling in the middle of the road for a moment and then he started picking up speed. When the bridge came into view, Tony turned on his siren and his flashers, and then he went a little blind. A white light, starting in the center, spread to the black edges of his sight. The speedometer read 80 . . . 90 . . . He saw his life unfurl like a perfect wave just as the cruiser slammed into the abutment of His Honor's bridge.

The sound of the crash could be heard for miles.

* * *

EPILOGUE

Mary Fletcher Rockwell stepped out from her front door in her bathrobe, picked up the *Parkdale Sunday News* and shook the light coating of snow from its plastic bag. It had been just about two years since the robbery at Gordon's and during that time she had learned a lot about herself and life in general. In the kitchen, she poured a cup of coffee for Jimmy and one for herself as she scanned the headlines.

Man's Nightmare Costs Radcliff New Jersey Over $ 1.6 Million: City Found Guilty in False Arrest Case after Turning Engineer's Life Upside Down.

BYLINE: Wayne Tinkle: *Trenton Tribune*

The city of Radcliff has been ordered to pay $ 1,663,314 in damages in a false-arrest case, in which a respected engineer was falsely charged as a jewel thief.

When his nightmare began two years ago, Eric Nordblum, originally of Tolleson, New Jersey, had top security clearance with MTS, a military technical systems company working on secret projects for the federal government. Nordblum's world was turned upside down when he was arrested on charges of taking part in a scam that featured switching fake diamond rings for genuine ones at Gordon's International department stores in Connecticut, New York, and New Jersey.

According to his lawyer, Attorney Frank V. Delmar, an associate with the Trenton law firm of Delmar and Meissener, Nordblum had never been in a Gordon's store and yet the police ignored his attempt to prove it.

The charges against Nordblum were dropped six months after his arrest because of insufficient evidence, but fighting the case cost him $ 63,000 in legal fees. More than a year later, he sued the City of Radcliff, Detective Bernard Pigeon, Radcliff's Police Chief Daniel Fortini, and Detective Anthony Deluca, who died in a tragic accident when his car crashed into the Deluca Bridge on his way home from this trial.

The U.S. District Court jury in Trenton awarded Nordblum $ 1,663,314, one of the largest police misconduct awards, not based on physical abuse, in New Jersey history. Radcliff's new City Attorney, Kevin Obonovitch, said this week that, while the city agreed not to appeal the award, it did not mean that it agreed with the jury's verdict. Police still maintain, as they did at the trial, that because they obtained an arrest warrant from a disinterested judge, there was nothing constitutionally wrong about arresting Nordblum.

Specifically, in the matter of *Eric Nordblum v. the Estate of Anthony A. Deluca*, individually and as a Radcliff police detective, the jury found in favor of the plaintiff in the sum of $100,000 for compensatory damages and $420,000 for punitive damages.

In the matter of *Eric Nordblum v. Bernard Pigeon*, individually and as a Radcliff police detective, the jury found in favor of the plaintiff in the sum of $100,000 for compensatory damages and $420,000 for punitive damages.

In the matter of *Eric Nordblum v. Daniel Fortini*, individually and in his official capacity as Chief of the Radcliff Police Department, the jury found in favor of the plaintiff in the sum of $80,000 for compensatory damages and $480,000 for punitive damages.

In the matter of *Eric Nordblum v. the city of Radcliff, New Jersey*, the jury found in favor of the plaintiff in the sum of $63,314 for compensatory damages.

Immediately following the announcement of this verdict, Anthony Deluca's father, His Honor Angelo Deluca, withdrew from the mayoral race, Daniel Fortini stepped down from his position as Chief of Radcliff Police, and Detective Bernard Pigeon resigned from the force.

Nordblum, contacted yesterday at his home in Woodmere, Long Island, New York, said: "No comment."

END

✳ ✳ ✳

READING GROUP GUIDE

Questions for discussion

1. The novel opens with a mysterious scene. How does this set up the tone for the rest of the book? Did it bother you that the thieves were never developed as key characters?

2. Relationships drive most of the central characters. Do you think Shelly and Eric's marriage would have survived had it not been for his arrest? Could you identify with Eric's downward spiral? Did you feel sorry for Shelly?

3. What are some of the recurring challenges that Tony faces in his relationship with his father? Was His Honor's suspicion that Tony was not really his son believable, and did you think it justified his disdain for Tony, or was something else going on?

4. Could you relate to Mary's fear for her job when she was involved in the robbery? How do you think she felt about herself when she was manipulated first by Tony and then by Eric?

5. Dan lived his whole life in Angelo's shadow. Do you think he disapproved of Angelo and might actually have been jealous of him? Do you think he knew that Tony was fabricating evidence and if so, why didn't he stop him?

6. Bernie was Tony's best friend since childhood. Were you surprised and/or disappointed when he betrayed Tony? What do you think motivated him to do such a thing?

7. Were you frustrated when Eric took so long to get angry and to take steps in his own defense? Do you wish the author had written more about his confrontation with Mary or was it enough just to know that she changed her story?

8. At what point did you suspect that it was with Maggie that Eric had the affair? Was her continued support of him believable even though they were not intimate again until the end of the book?

9. Was His Honor giving Tony a specific message or permission when he said: "no matter what"? Can you pinpoint the moment when Tony first crossed the line? Did you anticipate more lies from that moment on? Did you pity him for the position he had placed himself in?

10. Do you think that reckless indifference to the rights of an individual on the part of our legal system is

improving or getting out of control? Have you ever been accused of something you did not do?

Prepared by Shirley Phillips of H.C. Center

✶ ✶ ✶

If you wish to write a review of this novel, please enter: **Reckless Indifference** on: www.amazon.com and then scroll down to: "write an online review."

Made in the USA